P9-CFS-351

Bedford Free Public Library
Bedford, Massachusetts 01730

Home of the Bedford Flag

The Bedford Flag, commissioned to Cornet John Page in 1737 by King George II of England, was carried by his son, Nathaniel, who fought with the Bedford Minutemen at the Battle of Concord Bridge, April 19, 1775.

APR   2009

"NAMELESS DETECTIVE" MYSTERIES BY BILL PRONZINI

SCHEMERS

SCHEMERS

A Nameless Detective Novel

Bill Pronzini

A Tom Doherty Associates Book
New York

This is a work of fiction. All of the characters, organizations, and events portrayed in this novel are either products of the author's imagination or are used fictitiously.

SCHEMERS: A NAMELESS DETECTIVE NOVEL

Copyright © 2009 by the Pronzini-Muller Family Trust

All rights reserved.

A Forge Book
Published by Tom Doherty Associates, LLC
175 Fifth Avenue
New York, NY 10010

www.tor-forge.com

Forge® is a registered trademark of Tom Doherty Associates, LLC.

Library of Congress Cataloging-in-Publication Data

Pronzini, Bill.
    Schemers : a Nameless Detective novel / Bill Pronzini.—1st ed.
        p. cm.
    "A Tom Doherty Associates book."
    ISBN-13: 978-0-7653-1819-0
    ISBN-10: 0-7653-1819-9
    1. Nameless Detective (Fictitious character)—Fiction. 2. Private investigators—California—San Francisco—Fiction. 3. San Francisco (Calif.)—Fiction. 4. Rare books—Fiction. 5. Book thefts—Fiction. 6. Stalkers—Fiction. I. Title.
    PS3566.R67S38 2009
    813'.54—dc22

                                                    2008038102

First Edition: April 2009

Printed in the United States of America

0 9 8 7 6 5 4 3 2 1

For Rod Zimmerman,
good friend and fellow bookman
for half a century

ACKNOWLEDGMENTS

My thanks to Michael Seidman, for his valuable editorial and photography suggestions; to Joe Chernicoff, for once again sharing his knowledge of firearms; to Rod Zimmerman, for resolving my pharmaceutical dilemma; and to Marcia, for being there.

SCHEMERS

PROLOGUE

SCHEMER

The cemetery was just outside the Los Alegres city limits, big, sprawling, divided into older and newer sections built on rolling slopes. Plenty of trees and ground cover throughout. No night caretaker, no regular patrols, only a few night lights widely spaced. Gates locked at night, but the fences around it were six feet high and not topped by anything dangerous. Country road that ran along the front mostly deserted after midnight. No side roads. No houses anywhere in the vicinity. One tree-shadowed turnout toward the west end where you could park without worry of being noticed.

He rolled on past the gates, slow. Two-twenty a.m., nobody on the road, every light stationary. This was the third time he'd been out here this late. Three other trips during the day to pinpoint the family plot and to memorize the routes through the grounds. Ready as he'd ever be. Tonight was the night.

He felt good. A little excited, but it was tamped down. Calm. Controlled. Oh, he was *ready*—not just for the cemetery but for the rest of it to follow.

Turnout just ahead. Road still deserted. He shut off the headlights, swung in under the trees, silenced the engine. The backpack was on the seat beside him. He pulled it over onto his lap, held it gently when he got out, strapped it gently onto his back. Not much weight. One collapsible camping shovel, a pair of heavy gloves, two glass vials, and a cut length of cardboard didn't weigh much at all. The Kodak digital camera was in his jacket pocket. You could take decent photos with it—good resolution, good zoom, high ISO sensitivity. He preferred old-fashioned single-lens reflex cameras, but his old Nikkormat was too bulky to fit into the backpack.

Piece of cake, climbing the fence. He stayed in shape by watching what he ate, running five miles most days after work. But he made sure as he went up and over not to bump the backpack against the fence piping. The vials were pretty much unbreakable and he'd packed them in cotton batting, but he still had to be careful. Now, and in everything he did in the future. No mistakes.

Big shade tree not too far from the fence. He went over and stood under it, looking around, making sure of his bearings. Things looked different at night, the rows and shapes of grave markers big and small, the narrow gravel roads and footpaths that crisscrossed the cemetery. No moon tonight, but the sky was clear and there was enough starlight for him to see by. He'd always had good night vision.

Took him only a few seconds to locate the landmark he'd picked out: tall marble obelisk jutting up from the lawn in the newer section down here. It was maybe a hundred yards from where he stood. And from there, two hundred yards and ten degrees uphill to the Henderson plot in the older section. Easy.

He made his way toward the obelisk, crossing some of the graves, skirting others when there was a path to walk on. Some kind of bird made a noise; wind rustled tree branches; his steps set off little crunching sounds. Otherwise, stillness. Down below and behind him, the country road stayed empty.

Five or six minutes and he was at the Henderson plot. He recognized it, all right, even in the darkness, but he made sure anyway. Leaned up close to the six-by-four granite monument, shaded the beam of his pencil flash with his hand, and clicked it on just long enough to read the engraving.

LLOYD HENDERSON
1933–2004
BELOVED FATHER

Beloved. Jesus!

Rage boiled up in him. He had to stop himself from kicking the stone. Control, man, control. Too bad the marker was so goddamn big and heavy, cemented into the ground, otherwise he'd've yanked it out or knocked it over. Smashed it to bits with a sledgehammer, that's what he'd've liked to do, except that that would make too much noise.

He spat on it instead, as he had each time before.

Spat on the grave below it.

Then he took off the backpack, brought out the pair of heavy gloves and the shovel, and began to dig.

Didn't take him long. The earth under a layer of sod grass was loamy, easy to scoop into. Henderson had been cremated, the urn with his ashes planted here, and gravediggers didn't go down very deep when they were burying an urn. The shovel blade clanked on it and he dug it out, picked it up. Spat on it and laid it down next to the hole. Opened the backpack again and took out the two vials and unscrewed the cap on the smaller one. Slow and careful, slow and careful.

He bent forward, legs spread and feet planted, and extended the vial over the urn, just about an inch above it. Then he let the acid spill out.

It made a hissing sound, like a snake, as it ate into the bronze. Vapor came up, stinking. He stepped back. Kind of a wild laugh in his throat, but he didn't let it come out. Calm. Don't ever let yourself lose your cool.

But he said out loud what he was thinking. Had to say it, had to let that much come out.

"You son of a bitch," he said, "now *you're* burning for sure!"

To the backpack again for the second, larger vial. Opened that one, stepped cautiously around the smoking, burning remains of Lloyd fucking Henderson, leaned toward the monument in the same stance as before, and hurled the acid at the smooth granite face.

More hissing, more stinking vapors.

The name, the dates, the words "Beloved Father" began to disappear.

Now for the pix. One of the smoldering urn and ashes, one of the burning headstone. He made sure the road below was still deserted before he leaned up to shoot. Didn't have enough time to make each one perfect, not that he could have done that anyway with the digital camera, but it had a fairly sophisticated light meter built in, and you could count on the electronic flash to work every time.

Almost done. One more thing, the final touch—the sign that would let the rest of them know what they were in for. Do it quick, he'd been here long enough. But his hands inside the gloves felt itchy, dirty. There was a water tap on the lane nearby that he'd spotted the first time he came here; he went to it, washed his hands as best he could without soap. Should've thought to bring a bar along with him. Well, it wouldn't be long until he was back at the motel. Do a proper job then.

He flap-dried his hands, eased them back into the gloves. Then he took the piece of cardboard from the backpack, unfolded it, propped it against the low cement border at the front of the plot. He'd thought about adding one of his initials at the bottom, but there was no need for that. It wouldn't mean anything to them. The five words he'd painted in big bloodred letters were enough.

THIS IS JUST THE BEGINNING

Damn straight, he thought.

He caught up the backpack, spat once more on what was left of the gravesite, and made his way, slow and careful, back to the van.

1

Damp February Monday. And a day for oddball cases.

Mostly the jobs the agency takes on are pretty straight-forward, pretty routine. Insurance claims investigations, skip traces, employee background checks, domestic matters not involving divorce, finding and collecting from deadbeats of one stripe or another, information gathering for lawyers on criminal and civil cases. But now and then something unusual comes along to spice things up. Not often two in the same day, however.

The first of the pair on this Monday came by phone shortly after ten o'clock, from an unexpected and less than pleasing source. I was manning the South Park offices because Tamara wasn't. My partner is the agency's nerve center, a twenty-six-year-old technology expert and human dynamo who keeps it running smoothly and efficiently. With me and my limited computer skills in charge, it clanks along at about three-quarters power. Since my semiretirement I try to work only two or three days a week, and Monday isn't one of them, but Tamara had called me at home before breakfast and asked if I'd cover for her, she wouldn't be in until around noon, she'd tell me the reason when she saw me. I figured it must have something to do with the new flat on Potrero Hill she'd just moved into; something pleasurable, in any case, judging from the sunny sound of her voice.

When I answered the first call, a woman's voice asked for me by name. I owned up, and she said, "Margot Lee, Mr. Rivera's assistant at Great Western Insurance. Mr. Rivera would like to see you on a business matter, if you're available."

I was silent for so long she said, "Hello? Are you there?"

"I'm here," I said. "What sort of business matter?"

"A claim investigation, of course. Mr. Rivera would prefer to discuss the details in person."

"With me personally?"

"That's what he said, yes."

"When and where?"

"One o'clock today, here in his office, if that's convenient."

I almost said no, I wasn't interested. But I couldn't quite get the words out. An olive branch, maybe? Probably not; Barney Rivera wasn't given to offering olive branches to anybody. Must be a genuine business proposition. Why, all of a sudden, after five years?

"*Would* one o'clock be convenient?" Ms. Lee said.

"It would," I said before I could change my mind. "I'll be there."

Barney Rivera, Great Western's chief claims adjuster. Barney the Needle. We'd been friends once, poker buddies, and he'd thrown a fair amount of business my way in the days when I was running a one-man agency. That had all ended five years ago. Rivera had a malicious streak in him; he could be a gossip-mongering, backstabbing son of a bitch when he felt like it. He'd felt like it with me at a difficult time, when Kerry and I were going together and things were a little rocky and she'd thought maybe it wasn't me she wanted to be with but a guy named Blessing, the head of one of her ad agency's accounts. Rivera had seen them together at a restaurant and through sly, nasty innuendo implied to me that they were having a hot and heavy affair. They weren't—she never slept with Blessing—but Rivera's jabs had given me a bad time for a while. I'd never forgiven him. And when I turned down a couple of job offers afterward, he'd quit offering and I hadn't heard from him again until today. And not directly, at that. Just like the little bastard to have his assistant make initial contact.

Five years. A long time. And now, out of the blue what sounded like it could be a legitimate job offer. The "why" I couldn't figure at all.

I was mulling it over, and brooding a little about that rough patch in Kerry's and my relationship, when Jake Runyon came in. Good man, Jake—a former Seattle cop and former investigator for Caldwell & Associates, one of the larger private agencies up there. Big, slab-faced, hammer-jawed. Smart, tough, loyal, and dead-bang honest. He'd moved to San Francisco after the cancer death of his second wife, to be close to the estranged son from his first marriage, the only family he had left. They were still estranged; an attempt at reconciliation hadn't worked out.

For the first year he'd been with us as field operative, Runyon had been a reticent loner still grieving deeply for his deceased wife. Lately, though, there'd been a subtle change in him. Less dour, more open and upbeat. He'd even shaved off his mustache, as if he were making an effort to alter his physical appearance. Reason: a woman named Bryn Darby. He wouldn't say much about her or the nature of their relationship, and Tamara and I had yet to meet her, but it was plain that she was having a positive influence on him.

He had a light caseload this week, a fact that didn't set well with him. The restless type, Jake, uncomfortable unless he was on the move somewhere. So he'd come in hoping we had some work for him. I had to tell him no, though maybe the appointment with Barney the Needle would produce something for him to handle. We bulled a little, he went out to his desk in the anteroom, and I went back to the report I was writing.

And a short while later, oddball case number two showed up in person.

I heard them come in, a man and a woman, and the low buzz of conversation as Runyon spoke with them. Then he came into my office, shutting the door behind him. "Couple named Henderson, Tracy and Cliff," he said. "From Los Alegres. I think you should talk to them."

"What's their problem?"

"They're being stalked, but they don't know who or why."

"Stalked? They been to the police?"

He nodded. "No help there so far."

"If the police can't help them . . ."

"I know. But they sound pretty desperate."

"Well, we can listen to their story. You want to sit in?"

"Yes."

The Hendersons were in their late thirties, married thirteen years, with two young daughters. He was balding, rangy, tense, the owner of a construction company in Los Alegres, a small town some forty miles north of the city; she was blond, a little on the plump side and wearing clothes designed to diminish the fact, and a teacher of English and American history at the local high school. The look in her eyes was one I'd seen too many times before—a stunned-animal mix of hurt, fear, bewilderment, desperation. His eyes reflected more frustrated anger than anything else. Ordinary people suddenly and inexplicably threatened by extraordinary circumstance.

Once they were settled in the client chairs, and Runyon had taken up a position against the wall beside my desk, Tracy Henderson said, "I know we should have made an appointment, but after what happened last night . . . Well, we decided we should see someone as soon as possible."

"One of Los Alegres cops gave us your name," Cliff Henderson said.

"Lieutenant Adam St. John. He said your agency has a very good reputation."

I didn't know St. John. But when you've been in the

business as long as I have, and have had enough—too much—publicity on some cases, word gets around and police, lawyers, other professionals remember your name.

I said, "I understand you're being stalked."

"My brother Damon and me," Henderson said. "That much we're sure of."

"By an unknown party?"

"Unknown, and for no damn reason anybody can figure out."

"Stalked in what way?"

"Different ways, frightening ways," Mrs. Henderson said. "The night before last it got really ugly."

"Damon's in the hospital," Henderson said, "with a cracked head and a busted collarbone."

"What happened?"

"Attacked in his garage, middle of the night. Caught the bastard in there and got belted with a tire iron. He's lucky to be alive."

Runyon asked, "When did this trouble start?"

"Two and a half weeks ago. First thing he did, whoever he is, was vandalize our cemetery plot. My father's grave." A fierce anger darkened Henderson's face at the memory. "Got in there in the middle of the night and dug up the urn with Dad's ashes, poured acid all over it. Acid, for Christ's sake. Destroyed the headstone the same way."

"And he left a crude red-lettered sign," Mrs. Henderson said. " 'This is just the beginning.' "

"Cops thought at first it was random vandalism. But no other grave was vandalized that night or any night since."

I asked what else had happened.

"He trashed one of my job sites," Henderson said. "Paint, acid all over the place. Dumped more acid on my truck, parked right in our driveway. Damon's car, too. Then that garage break-in . . . Christ knows what he would've done in there if Damon hadn't heard him and run out."

"Did he get a look at the man?"

"No. Too dark, happened too fast. Bastard hit him from behind, straddled him, broke his collarbone with another swing. Damon thought he was a dead man. But the guy said something like 'Not yet, it's not time yet' and got off him and beat it."

"Is that all that was said?"

"That's all."

"Has he contacted either of you in any way? E-mails, letters, anonymous phone calls?"

"No. Just that sign at the cemetery." Henderson's fingers clenched and unclenched, as if he were flexing them around the perp's neck. "Crazy. No damn reason for any of it."

"And you know of no one who might have a grudge against you and your brother?"

Mrs. Henderson said, "No, absolutely not. That's what's so frightening."

Runyon asked, "A business deal where a third party felt wronged in some way?"

"We thought of that," Henderson said, "but that can't be it. He's after both Damon and me and we've never done a business deal together with anybody, not even each other."

"What does your brother do for a living?"

"CPA. Small practice, mainly local businesses. Never a hassle with any of his clients. Never a hassle with anybody I've worked with, either."

"The cemetery vandalism was two and a half weeks ago, you said. Did anything unusual happen around that time, or in the month or so before? An accident of some kind, an altercation, even a few harsh words with somebody—anything that might have triggered this man's rage?"

"No. I've racked my brains, we all have, and there's nothing. Nothing. We live quiet, do our jobs, go to church, raise our kids the best way we know how, don't get on anybody's wrong side. A faceless enemy like that . . . I don't know, I just don't know."

"We have two daughters, nine and thirteen," his wife said. "Damon has a son, twelve. What if this lunatic decides to go after one of them? We're at our wits' end."

"The cops have sent out patrols to keep an eye on our homes and businesses. But they can't watch twenty-four seven."

I said, "If you're looking to hire bodyguards . . ."

"No. Not yet, anyway, not unless there's a threat to the kids. We've made our own arrangements to protect them for now. An investigation's what we want. Thorough, not the kind the cops are giving us."

"A fresh perspective," Mrs. Henderson said.

"I understand. But I have to be honest with you. There may not be a great deal we or any other private agency can do."

"Are you saying you won't help us?"

"Not at all. We'll investigate, but in a case like this, with so little information to go on . . ."

"We don't expect miracles," Henderson said. "Just do what you can, that's all we're asking."

I laid out our standard fees, as well as the probable expense account charges, and the amount required as a retainer. The figures didn't seem to faze them. I had them sign an agency contract, and Tracy Henderson wrote out a check. Then I took down two pages of names, addresses, phone numbers, personal information—everything we'd need to open an investigation.

Runyon's body language said that he wanted the job, so I told the clients he'd be handling it. Henderson asked when we'd start. Runyon said he'd drive up to Los Alegres this afternoon.

Solemn handshakes, and they were gone.

Runyon said then, "Phantom stalkers are the worst kind. And this one sounds unstable as hell. Okay if we make the investigation a priority?"

"I think we'd better. Can you shuffle your schedule for the rest of the week? Alex can cover for you if needs be." Alex Chavez, our part-time operative.

"Shouldn't be a problem."

"Okay. I'll photocopy my notes before you head for Los Alegres. And when Tamara gets here I'll have her get started on deep background checks on the Henderson brothers."

"Where is she anyway?"

"Took the morning off."

"That's not like her."

"No, it's not," I said. "She must have a good reason."

Good reason? Yes and no.

Tamara showed up at one minute past noon. Bounced straight into my office, high color in her cheeks, big cat-ate-the-canary smile, and announced, "Well, I finally got my groove back."

"Come again?"

"Oh, yeah," she said, grinning.

"Huh?"

"I finally got laid."

Well, what do you say to that? If she'd been a man, I might have made a mildly bawdy observation. As it was, all I could manage was a lame "Oh."

"Four times altogether," she said. "Last night and this morning."

"Uh."

"That's why I took the morning off. Been so long, I figured I was entitled."

"Mm."

"Almost a year since the last time, can you believe it? I'd almost forgotten what it feels like."

"Ah."

"His name's Lucas Zeller," she said. "I met him at Vonda's wedding reception, knows her brother James. Not exactly a brother himself, though."

"No?"

"Fudge swirl," she said.

"Huh?"

"Mostly dark with a little white mixed in. Like fudge swirl ice cream. Hot fudge sundae!"

The conversation was making me uncomfortable, as personal conversations with Tamara sometimes did. As outspoken and uninhibited as she was, she was liable to launch into a blow-by-blow—literally, God forbid—description of her evening and morning activities with the fudge swirl, and that was information I had no desire to tune in.

"Anyhow," she said then, sparing me, "nothing clicked between us that day at the reception, not for me, but Saturday he called up out of the blue, said he had tickets to the Zombie Boys concert yesterday—"

"The which?"

"Zombie Boys, they're a hard-rock blowout band, very cool, usually you can't get tickets."

"Ah."

"So I said sure. We went out to dinner first, then the blowout, then back to my place and the rest is sweet history. That man is something *fierce* in bed, you know what I'm saying?"

I said quickly, "Serious, you and this Lucas?"

"Doing the nasty is always serious when you haven't been doing it."

"You know what I mean. Potentially serious relationship."

"No way. I had enough of that with Horace. All I'm looking for is some fun, a little action. Lucas feels the same. Besides, I think maybe he's Mama's boy."

"Uh?"

"Thirty-four, salesman for a company that sells electronic

equipment, still lives with his mother. Can you believe it? She was all he talked about at dinner, what a great person she is, all that—almost spoiled the mood. But once we got between the sheets, Mama wasn't there anymore."

"I should hope not."

"Whooo! That man's a real dawg when it comes to—"

The telephone rang just then. Thank you, Lord, I thought.

The call was for me, a minor matter I disposed of in less than a minute. Tamara was still standing there, grinning and glowing, when I hung up. To forestall any more discussion of her sex life, I said, "Busy morning here, too, while you were playing. One new case and one surprise call, both oddball."

"How so?"

I told her, the Henderson business first, then about the call from Barney Rivera's assistant.

"Rivera, huh?" she said. "You think maybe he's up to one of his little tricks, for old times' sake?"

"I wouldn't put anything past him," I said. "Whatever he's up to, I'll know in about an hour. And it better be legitimate business. If it isn't, he'll be ingesting those peppermints of his through a different orifice than his mouth."

2

Barney the Needle hadn't changed much in half a decade. He kept me waiting for fifteen minutes before he sent his assistant out to fetch me, and as soon as I walked into his office he showed me his salesman's grin, pumped my hand, clapped me on the shoulder, and said I was looking pretty good for an old fart—all as if it had been five days instead of five years since we'd last laid eyes on each other.

We sat down and did some mutual measuring across his big blond-wood desk. He looked the same except for a little less hair and a little more gray at the temples of what was left—a roly-poly little bastard with a cherub's face, a pit bull's heart, and a borderline sadist's sense of humor. The same glass bowl of peppermints was on the desktop; he had an addiction to the things.

"So," he said, lacing his hands across his paunch. "Been quite a while."

"Yeah. Quite a while."

"Lots of happenings in your life since the last time we saw each other. Married, adopted a kid, took in a partner and expanded operations."

"Been keeping tabs, have you?"

"Nah. But word gets around."

"Then you know I'm semiretired now."

He chuckled. "Sure you are. Just like me. What'd you think of Margot?"

"Your assistant? Seems competent."

"Bet your ass." Wink, wink. "In the office and in bed, both."

I didn't say anything.

"No lie," he said. "I'm laying her."

Twice today, people telling me about their sex lives. I didn't mind it so much from Tamara. From Rivera, it set my teeth on edge. He might or might not have been BS'ing; he'd always had a certain amount of success with women, the type who need somebody to mother. He'd once told me he'd slept with over three hundred women in his life. Even if that were true, which I doubted, he'd had enough conquests to give legitimacy to his bragging. And brag he did, often, to anybody who'd listen, with no consideration whatsoever for the women's feelings or reputations.

He winked at me again and popped a peppermint, and I thought: You little prick, how could I have ever considered you a friend?

"You didn't crawl out of the woodwork after five years to tell me about you and your assistant," I said. "What is it you want, Barney?"

He wasn't offended. You couldn't offend him without the aid of a needle twice as big as the one he used. "A job I figured you'd be interested in," he said. "Soon as the claim came across my desk last Friday, I thought of you. Right up your alley."

"Why is that?"

"Has to do with books, for one thing. Rare books."

"I don't know anything about rare books."

"Collect them, don't you? Mystery books?"

"No, I collect pulp magazines. Big difference."

"Valuable, though, right? Old and valuable."

"I suppose so. In the collector's market."

"The policyholder in this case collects vintage first-edition mysteries dating back more than a hundred years. Owns some fifteen thousand volumes, appraised at more than seven million and insured for that amount."

"You're kidding."

"Nope. His collection's one of the three or four largest in the world."

"He must be a multimillionaire."

"Inherited money. His old man was the inventor of some gadget used in early jet planes. He's been with Great Western for twenty years, one of our biggest clients—personal property, accident, three life policies. Never missed a payment on any of them, never filed a claim before this one."

"And this one is for?"

"Eight books allegedly stolen from his library a week ago," Rivera said, "worth a cool half a million bucks."

"Eight books, half a million?"

Rivera used his computer to consult the case file. "*The Adventures of Sherlock Holmes,* Arthur Conan Doyle, British first edition. *The Maltese Falcon* and *Red Harvest,* Dashiell Hammett. *The Big Sleep,* Raymond Chandler. *The Postman Always Rings Twice,* James M. Cain. *The Roman Hat Mystery,* Ellery Queen. *The Murder of Roger Ackroyd,* Agatha Christie, British. *Fer-de-Lance,* Rex Stout. All inscribed and signed copies in dust jackets except the Doyle and Christie."

"My God," I said.

"Impressed, huh?"

"From what I know, those are not only rare first editions but virtually impossible to replace even for a multimillionaire."

"That's what Pollexfen says. Gregory Pollexfen. Name mean anything to you?"

Poll-*ex*-fen. Odd name. "No. Where does he live?"

"Right here in the city. Sea Cliff."

"He must be beside himself. I would be if some of my rarest pulps had been swiped."

"If the books were swiped," Rivera said.

"If?"

"There's some question about that. That's how come you're here."

"Why doubt him, if he's been such a good risk for twenty years?"

"The books were taken from his locked library, he says. Double locks on all the windows and the only door, a special security alarm on his house."

"Who else has access to the library? Wife, children?"

"Two other people live in the house—his wife, her brother. A secretary and a housekeeper come in weekdays. But according to Pollexfen, none of them is allowed in the library except in his presence. Same with fellow bibliophiles and any other visitors."

"And I suppose he's the only one with a key to the library."

"According to him."

"Keys can get stolen or misplaced or copied."

"He says that couldn't have happened."

"So if the books really were stolen . . ."

"Right, the only person who could've done it was Pollexfen. Which he vehemently denies, of course."

"If he's lying, why make up a story like that? There're dozens of more plausible explanations."

"The circumstances, maybe," Rivera said. "Library locked up and nobody else with access."

"That doesn't quite fly. He could've convinced the rest of the household to lie about the security precautions."

"Unless he figured they wouldn't go along or he couldn't trust them."

I said, "Only one reason I can think of why a passionate collector would steal from himself and then file an insurance claim."

"Sure. He needs the half mil. Except that Pollexfen *doesn't* need it. He's as financially solid as a rock."

"But you still don't want to give him the benefit of the doubt."

"With a half mil payoff at stake? Hell no. Not without a full investigation. Which he says he welcomes. Send out the best investigator we've got, he said. But I thought of you anyway."

I let that pass. "Did Pollexfen file a police report?"

"Right away. They haven't found zip. Incompetents, Pollexfen called them. He's probably right on that score. What do cops know about rare books?"

"He told you the books were stolen a week ago, but his claim came in last Friday. Why the delay?"

"Waiting to see what the police turned up."

"All right. Assuming the books were stolen, does Pollexfen have any idea who did it or how it was done?"

"Nope. It's impossible, he says, and yet it happened." Another peppermint disappeared into the Rivera maw. "Hey, I just had a thought. Maybe it was the Invisible Man."

I ignored that, too.

"Locked room, impossible crime—you got lucky with that kind of thing a couple of times, as I recall. That's the second reason you're here. If somebody besides Pollexfen did manage to five-finger eight valuable books from a locked library, you're the only genius I know who can figure out how it was done."

Genius. Sure. The needle again.

He sat there sucking on the peppermint, grinning at me—a grin with an edge of malice. The smug bastard had me hooked and he knew it. And he didn't waste any time saying so.

"Irresistible, eh?"

"Depends. What're you offering for the job?"

"Usual rates."

"Ours have gone up in five years. We don't come cheap anymore."

He shrugged. "I don't mind inflation."

"You're one of the few who doesn't."

"Tell you what, old buddy. If you find those missing books and save us the half mil, I'll authorize a bonus for you."

"How much of a bonus?"

"Oh, say two thousand."

I said without missing a beat, "Let's make it five."

"Man, you really have gotten greedy in your old age."

"People change in five years. Some people."

"Not me. Still the same old Barney."

"Yeah."

"So okay then. Five thousand."

"Put it in writing and we've got a deal."

No argument. He put it in writing, all cheerful and smiley.

Barney the Needle, Barney the Sly. He was so damn accommodating because he figured I'd never collect that five thousand bonus—he expected me to fail. That was the real reason he'd brought me in here after five years. To have the last laugh.

Barney the Shit.

Tamara said, "Five K bonus? Sweet."

"If I can find those first editions."

"Anybody can, you the man."

"Screwy case. I should've turned Rivera down, bonus or no bonus."

"But you didn't. Too much of a challenge, right?"

"There's that. And the prospect of putting the needle right back into his tubby hide. I'd settle for that."

"Want me to do a b.g. on Pollexfen?"

"If you have time. The Henderson case takes priority. You come up with anything there yet?"

"So far," she said, "nothing that flies against what they told you about themselves and the brother. No criminal records of any kind, no juicy stuff. Just average folks, looks like."

"Who are being systematically stalked. The attacks are too personal to be random. Has to be a motive of some kind."

"Psychos don't need much to get off on."

"No, but they do need a trigger. Just about everybody has secrets, past problems of some kind. I doubt the Henderson family is an exception."

In my office I went through the printouts Rivera had given me: copies of Gregory Pollexfen's seven-million-dollar book collection policy and claim, information on his other policies, personal data. Pollexfen must be financially solid; he was putting five figures a year in premiums into the Great Western coffers. Age: two months shy of his sixty-eighth birthday. Health: subpar. Heart ailment, high blood pressure, other maladies that, combined with his age, had sent his life insurance premiums skyrocketing the past couple of years. His present wife, Angelina, number three after a pair of divorces, was thirty-two years his junior. Married to her nine years, no children by her or the other two wives. The interesting thing there was that she was no longer the named beneficiary of his life insurance policy; he'd crossed her out three years ago in favor of two major charities. And his was the only name on the general personal property and book collection policies.

Why? I wondered. If the marriage was rocky enough to cause him to change beneficiaries, then it was likely he'd written her out of his will, too, leaving her with no more than the standard spousal death benefits required by state law. But if that was the case, why were they still living together?

After I'd familiarized myself with everything, I put in a call to Pollexfen's home. He was there; the woman who answered the phone went and got him for me.

"I've been waiting to hear from you. Mr. Rivera called a little while ago, gave me your name." Froggy baritone that cracked a little here and there. "He said you're exactly the right investigator for this case."

"Uh-huh."

"He also told me," Pollexfen said, "that you collect pulp magazines."

"That's right."

"For how many years?"

"More than I care to remember."

"How many do you own?"

"Around seven thousand."

"Rarities? The *Maltese Falcon* issues of *Black Mask*?"

"All five, yes."

"Excellent! I know I'm going to enjoy meeting you."

"What would be a convenient time for me to come by?"

"I'm completely free this afternoon."

"Three o'clock?"

"Excellent," he said again. "You have the address, of course."

"I have it."

"I'll expect you at three then."

I put the phone down. "I know I'm going to enjoy talking to you," he'd said. Odd choice of words under the circumstances. But then, collectors, honest or otherwise, are all a little cracked. Myself included.

3

JAKE RUNYON

He'd been to Los Alegres before, once on business, once on one of his periodic drives to familiarize himself with his new home territory, so he had no trouble finding his way around. It was a valley town, spread out between low foothills; former agricultural center founded in the 1850s, now a combination bedroom community, site for upscale business enterprises, and haven for writers, artists, and professional people attracted by the historic downtown, big old west-side homes, the saltwater estuary that terminated in its midst. Population around fifty thousand, most of that number in sprawling developments on the east side.

The police station was on North Main, housed in a gray cinderblock building that looked more like a converted mortuary than a cop house and sided by a fenced-in yard where the patrol cars and other vehicles were kept. Runyon ID'd himself to the woman sergeant at the front desk and outlined the reason he was there. That and one of his business cards got him in to see Lieutenant Adam St. John.

St. John was in his fifties, lean and fox-faced, with tired eyes and a slow way of moving as if he were trying to conserve energy. He seemed to need to make it clear at the outset that bringing in a private investigative service on the Henderson case wasn't his idea.

"I told them that if we can't do anything, it's damn unlikely anybody else can. But they insisted. Your agency's got a good rep, so I handed out your name." He shrugged. "It's their money."

"Pretty desperate, from what they told us."

"Can't blame them for that. If I had some whack job after me, I guess I'd be desperate, too."

"Any new developments?"

"Not yet. We've done everything we can, and then some. It's not like we're trying to slough off on this." Now he was on the defensive.

"Nobody thinks that," Runyon said.

"Yeah, well, it's frustrating for us, too. I mean, there's just nothing to go on. Nothing in the family's background, at least nothing we can find or they're willing to talk about. We ran both brothers through the NCIS and even made an FBI inquiry. Zip."

"The father, too?"

"Lloyd Henderson? Why should we run his name?"

"His grave was vandalized."

"Vicious act aimed at the two sons," St. John said. "Hell, the man's been dead for years."

Runyon consulted his file notes. "Died in 2004."

"Right. Natural causes, in case you're wondering."

"What did he do for a living?"

"Dentist. Retired. Lived here all his life, served on the city council, belonged to the Rotary, Kiwanis, all the civic organizations. You won't find a more respected member of the community."

"Take your word for it," Runyon said. "The brother who was attacked in his garage. Damon, is it?"

"Damon, right."

"Anything he could tell you about the perp?"

"No. He had a flashlight, but he got hit from behind. All he saw was a shadow."

"Size estimate?"

"Big, from the weight when he was straddled."

"And all the perp said to him was 'Not yet, it's not time yet'?"

"That's all."

"He's sure about the words?"

"Positive."

"What about the voice? Anything distinctive?"

"No. Just a whisper. And he was hurting bad by then."

"What about olfactory impressions?"

"Olfactory . . . smells? You mean did the guy smell?"

"Body odor, cigarettes, booze, cologne or aftershave."

". . . Henderson didn't say anything about that."

And St. John hadn't thought to ask. Runyon let it go. "How did the perp get inside the garage?"

"Jimmied the lock on the side door. Didn't make much noise, but Henderson was awake—using the toilet. That's how come he heard."

"Perp wore gloves, I suppose. No prints."

"None that didn't belong to the family members."

"Other evidence of any kind?"

"Not that we could find." St. John was defensive again. "We don't have a big city forensics department here. We did the best we could."

"Sure you did," Runyon said. "What about Damon's family? They see or hear anything?"

"His wife woke up and ran out when she heard him screaming. But the perp was gone by then."

"Neighbors?"

"Woman lives down the block thought she heard a car racing off but she didn't see it. Otherwise . . . no."

"Damon still in the hospital?"

"As of this morning. He'll probably be there a couple more days. The perp busted up his collarbone pretty badly with that tire iron."

Runyon said, "That's about it for now, then. Thanks for your help, Lieutenant."

"Okay. Just make sure you let me know if you find out anything." The look in St. John's eyes said he'd be damn surprised if Runyon did.

Los Alegres Valley Cemetery was in a semirural area a couple of miles northeast of the Henderson residence. One look at the somewhat secluded location, the low encircling fence, and it was easy to see how the perp had gotten in and out without being seen. The main gates were open and when Runyon drove through he could see a couple of low buildings off on the right—office, maintenance facility. But he didn't need to go there to find out where the Henderson family plot was located. Two men working with a big forklift drew him to the other end of the grounds, and when he reached them he saw that they were putting a new black-granite monument into one of the larger sites—the Henderson plot, it turned out. Much of the earth in the large, square patch of ground had been dug up and resodded as well.

There were half a dozen gravestones in addition to the new monument with Lloyd Henderson's name on it. The others, judging from the names and dates, appeared to be the parents and grandparents of Lloyd Henderson, and two sisters who had predeceased him.

The older of the workmen, heavyset and gray-bearded, was supervising the job. Runyon approached him, flashed his license, explained what he was doing there. The man, Joe Sobolewsky, was head groundskeeper and willing to talk.

"I was the one found the mess in the morning," he said. He had a malleable face; it twisted up into an expression of disgust. "Never seen anything like it in all the years I been here. Close my eyes, I can still smell the stink of that acid."

"Extensive damage?"

"Real extensive. Enough acid on the marker to wipe out all the words, eat a hole in the granite big enough to put the top of your head in."

"Not simple vandalism, then."

"Oh, hell, no. We get that kind of thing out here once in a great while, but nothing like this."

"Hate crime," Runyon said.

"That's it, mister. That's it in a nutshell. Hate crime."
Sobolewsky paused to dig a knuckle into one ear. "One
funny thing," he said.

"What's that?"

"Water tap over there on your right. When I came out
that morning, the ground under it was soaking wet. And
it wasn't from leakage—the tap was shut off tight."

"As if somebody turned it on for some reason during
the night."

"Right. Had to be the guy who desecrated the grave.
But I can't figure why, unless all that devil's work made
him thirsty."

"Or he spilled a drop or two of acid on himself or his
clothing."

"Yeah, that could be it, too."

Runyon asked, "Do you know the Hendersons?"

"Not personally. By reputation. Good people."

"So you don't know of anyone who'd have this much
of a grudge against one or more of the family?"

"I sure don't. Cops asked me that, too. Beats the hell
out of me."

"Whoever did it had to have come here at least once and
probably two or three times," Runyon said. "Pinpoint the
location, figure out how to find his way in the dark."

"Sounds reasonable."

"You see anybody in this vicinity before it happened? At
any time?"

"No, nobody," Sobolewsky said. "Frank, neither,
he's my assistant there on the forklift. But I work all over
these grounds—maintenance, landscaping, grave-digging.

People come and go, put down flowers, pay their respects. Me and Frank, we're both too busy to pay much attention unless somebody does something, you know, out of the ordinary."

"And nobody did."

"If somebody had, we'd've sure told the cops when they asked."

As much as he hated hospitals, after all the time he'd spent in Seattle General watching Colleen waste away to a morphined husk, Runyon seemed to find himself in one too damned often since he'd moved down here. Once in Red Bluff as a patient, the mild concussion on the firebug business last September. As a visitor when his son's boyfriend had been mugged and badly beaten in the city, twice more in Red Bluff, and now again in Los Alegres.

They were all the same. Same sounds, same smells, same palpable aura of sickness and death. Took a special kind of person to be a doctor or a nurse or any other kind of hospital worker, people with systems immune to the stifling atmosphere—total opposites of a man like him, who needed to be outdoors and moving. Walls, particularly hospital walls, had a way of closing in on him after a while. As soon as he walked through the main entrance of Los Alegres Valley Hospital, he felt his stomach contract and his gorge rise, and the images of Colleen shriveled in that white bed in that white room came flooding back with an impact that was almost physical. Not as intense a reaction now as it had been, but bad enough.

A woman on the reception desk told him where to

find Damon Henderson. He rode an elevator up to the second floor, followed directions to the south wing. It was an old building with three or four wings, a couple of them probably add-ons, surrounded by medical offices, shopping centers, older east-side tracts. Everything was clean, reasonably well maintained, but faintly shabby, and the equipment struck him as borderline obsolete. The hospital stink seemed stronger up here; tightening his nasal passages and breathing through his mouth didn't block it out. There was muscle tension all through him by the time he got to the semiprivate room where Damon Henderson lay and a woman sat in a chair at his bedside, holding his hand.

The man—early to midthirties, slight, balding like his brother—was in rough shape. Facial bruises and contusions, right arm and shoulder in a cast. Doped to relieve his pain, apparently, but alert enough to talk. The thin-faced, scared-looking woman was his wife, Samantha. They were expecting him; Cliff had called her from San Francisco, she said, then stopped in at the hospital after he got back to tell Damon.

Runyon asked the same questions he'd asked Lieutenant St. John, got pretty much the same answers. All except one. When he asked Damon Henderson if he'd had any aural or olfactory impressions of his attacker, the man said, "I've been thinking about that. Yes. Soap."

"How do you mean exactly? His body, his clothing?"

"Everything about him. One of his hands, on my neck . . . gloved, but the soap smell was still strong."

"As if he'd scrubbed up recently."

"Yes. His hair . . . shampoo. And his clothes . . . freshly washed. Heavy, sweetish smell."

"Dryer sheets?" his wife said.

"That's it. All the odors were so strong it was almost . . . I don't know, I was in so much pain . . ."

What kind of man washes himself, shampoos his hair, and puts on clean clothes to break into a garage in the middle of the night? Somebody with OCD, maybe. Compulsive hand washer, cleanliness freak. That might explain the wet ground under the cemetery water tap, too.

Runyon said as much and then asked, "Do you know anyone who fits that description? Obsessive-compulsive about cleanliness?"

"I can't . . . no, I don't think so."

"Mrs. Henderson?"

"No. No one."

"Just a few more questions. Did you have an impression of the man's age?"

". . . Well, youngish, I think. From the sound of his voice."

"Twenties? Thirties?"

"I'm not sure—twenties, I guess."

"Anything distinctive about the voice?"

"Not that I can remember. The pain . . . it was right af-ter he clubbed me."

"Any idea of what he was doing in your garage?"

Henderson was tiring. His eyelids drooped, and when he tried to shift position, hurt twisted his mouth out of shape. "Sabotage my car again, I suppose."

"He'd already done that once?"

"In my office parking lot, one night when I was working late. Threw acid on the tires, all four of them."

"Was there any damage to anything in the garage?"

"No. He didn't have time . . . I was out there pretty fast after I heard him break in."

"Where did he come from when he hit you?"

"Where? I'm not . . . My left, over by my workbench."

"Keep anything flammable in that area? Paint thinner, gasoline?"

"No flammable liquids, but there's a lot of cardboard and paper—I store my old business files in the garage."

"Near the workbench."

"No, along the wall on the other side."

"My God," Mrs. Henderson said, "are you suggesting he might've been planning to set fire to our garage?"

"I'm not suggesting anything. Just asking questions. Would you mind if I had a look around the garage? The rest of your property?"

"The police have already been over everything. . . ."

"I'd like to see it for myself."

"Go ahead," Henderson said. "Anything you need."

"I'll be home in an hour or so," his wife said. "Unless you'd like to go there now . . ."

"No hurry. Later this afternoon is fine."

She drew a heavy breath. "Mr. Runyon, we have a twelve-year-old son. Cliff and Tracy have two young daughters. You *have* to find this man, find out who he is and why he's doing this to us, stop him before he . . ." The rest of it seemed to stick in her throat.

Runyon didn't believe in offering false assurances. But

these were desperate people. He said, "I'll do everything I can," and left them with that thin little thread of hope.

Perp possibly in his twenties, possibly with an obsessive-compulsive disorder. Not much to go on, without some idea of why he'd targeted the Hendersons. A man with a real or imagined hate-on for both of the brothers, or for the Henderson family. The father had been dead for five years, so it didn't figure to be him.

Still, the first act of aggression had been to burn Lloyd Henderson's ashes and the words off his monument with acid. Vicious and personal act. Everything else he'd done, with the exception of the assault on Damon Henderson, and that hadn't been planned, was mild by comparison.

Something to do with the father after all?

4

Cliff and Tracy Henderson lived on Walnut Street. Runyon looked up the location on the Los Alegres map he'd bought, found it on the west side not far from the town center. The address turned out to be an old, two-story house with a columned side porch shaded by a tulip tree. The yard on the other side was fenced. The reason for the fencing was apparent as soon as he started up the front walk: a big brown and black dog, some kind of rottweiler mix, came charging out of the back barking and growling. Good for the Hendersons. A loud and aggressive animal was the best kind of home protection they could have.

The dog kept up the racket as Runyon stood on the front porch thumbing the bell. No response. But as he came back down the steps, a dark gray SUV rolled upstreet and turned into the driveway. Tracy Henderson was at the wheel. He stood waiting as she and her passengers, two young girls, piled out.

51

"Oh, Mr. Runyon," she said. "Are you looking for Cliff? He's at a job site . . ."

"I'd like to talk to you, if you can spare a few minutes."

"Of course." The two girls came up, one on either side of her. She said, "My daughters, Shana and Rachel. I just picked them up at school."

The thirteen-year-old, Shana, gave him her hand in a solemn, grown-up way. The younger one, Rachel, said "Hello" shyly and stayed where she was, close to her mother. They knew who he was; their solemn expressions conveyed that. Good for the Hendersons on that score, too. You couldn't protect kids their age by trying to shield them from what was going on.

The dog was still barking. Mrs. Henderson yelled, "Thor! Quiet!" but the command didn't have much effect. "He's a good watchdog but once he gets started . . . Come inside, Mr. Runyon, we'll talk in the living room. Just let me get the girls settled in their rooms." She'd been calm enough in the agency offices this morning, but now she looked and acted frazzled. Worry and tension taking their toll.

She deposited him in a living room that ran most of the house's width across the front. Heavy dark furniture and rose-patterned wallpaper gave it the look of rooms you saw in movies made in the forties. Its focal points created a culture clash: shelves crammed with books along one wall, a television set displayed in front of one draped window. The TV won the clash hands down: ultra-modern fifty-two-inch flat-screen job on a long, high table, like a shrine to a false god. Runyon, waiting, stayed on his feet even though she'd invited him to sit down.

She was back in not much more than three minutes. "Would you like something to drink? Coffee, a soda?"

"Nothing, thanks."

"I'm going to have a small scotch. You don't mind? I don't usually drink this early, but . . ."

"I understand."

She poured the scotch neat, sipped it, made a face, sipped again as she lowered herself into one of a matching pair of overstuffed armchairs. The couch suited him; by turning sideways to face her, he had his back to the monster TV.

She said, "Are you here because you have something to tell us? Or is it more questions?"

"Questions, for now. Trying to cover all the possibilities."

"Yes, of course."

"I spoke to your brother-in-law in the hospital earlier." He told her what Damon Henderson had remembered about the perp. "Do you know anyone who fits that description? Young, compulsive about cleanliness?"

"No." Wry mouth. "Most of my students and some members of my family would fall into the opposite category."

Runyon said, "You're all convinced there's nothing your husband or his brother did or were involved in that triggered the stalker's rage. That opens up the possibility that the motive may not be directly related to them."

"What do you mean?"

"It could be a grudge against another member of the family."

"I don't see how that's possible. There aren't any other siblings. Or any close relatives except for an elderly aunt who lives in Florida."

"The first and most brutal attack was the desecration of their father's grave. That could be significant."

"You think . . . something against Lloyd? My Lord, he's been gone five years."

"What was the cause of his death?"

"Cancer. Esophageal." She winced and shook her head as she spoke. "It was a long and painful death, very difficult on all of us."

Flash memory of Colleen in the hospital bed, close to the end, her body and her face wasted, ninety-six pounds when she died . . . He put a block up against the memory, locked his mind against its return.

"Your husband and his brother were close to their father?"

"Oh, yes. Very close."

"What kind of man was he?"

"A good man. Warm, generous."

"Marks against him, trouble of any kind he might have had?"

"None that I ever knew about."

"Enemies, business or personal?"

Emphatic headshake. "Lloyd was a *dentist*. And very involved in the community. Men like that don't make enemies, any more than men like my husband and his brother do."

"Somebody made one somewhere, Mrs. Henderson."

"Yes. Yes, of course, but . . ." Words failed her; she shook her head and finished what was left in her glass.

"I stopped by the cemetery earlier," Runyon said. "No grave in the family plot for Cliff and Damon's mother."

"That's because she's still alive."

"Living where?"

"Assisted living facility in Sonoma. At least she was as of a year ago."

"So your husband doesn't have much contact with her."

"Almost none, as a matter of fact. She . . . well, neither Cliff nor Damon is close to her."

"Why is that?"

"Well, they blamed her for breaking up their family. They were just boys at the time, not much older than my girls, and it's natural for children to take sides in a bitter divorce."

"Why was it bitter?"

"Mona just decided one day that she'd had enough and was leaving. Blindsided poor Lloyd, evidently. Everyone suspected . . . well, another man. She married again as soon as her divorce was final, a plumber in Sonoma."

"Any children from that marriage?"

"No."

"Did she remain married to her second husband?"

"Until he died of a stroke about three years ago. Her health began to deteriorate afterward and that's when she went into the facility."

"What's the name of the facility? And her full name?"

"Sunset Acres. Mona Crandall. Are you planning to

talk to her? I can't imagine what she could possibly have to tell you."

"Neither can I, right now." Runyon made a note of the names. "I take it your father-in-law had plenty of friends. Who were the closest?"

"Well, Hayden Brock, for one. They played golf together every weekend. And Dr. George . . . George Thanapolous."

"Dentist or medical doctor?"

"Orthopedist. He's retired now. Hayden still practices law even though he's well into his seventies. His offices are downtown on Spring Street. Brock, Leland, and Brock."

Runyon added that information in his notebook.

"If you want to talk to Cliff," Mrs. Henderson said, "he should be home around five or so."

"Not necessary. You've given me all the information I need for now. You can fill him in on what we discussed."

The dog started barking again, long and loud, when he left the house. He could still hear it when he was half a block away, even with the car windows rolled up.

Samantha Henderson was waiting for him when he arrived at the home she shared with Cliff's brother, Damon. Development of tract houses in a country setting west of town—the custom-built, expensive variety on large lots with plenty of landscaping to give the illusion of privacy. Some enterprising developer's idea of gracious living, small-town version.

The two-car garage was detached, separated from the colonial-style house by a walkway and a narrow strip of ground planted with flowers and low-growing cypress shrubs. The door to the garage was on that side, not quite directly opposite a side door into the house. Mrs. Henderson stood by while Runyon examined the door. The lock wasn't much, just the standard push-button variety. It would have taken little effort to spring it with a credit card, much less a tire iron. But the perp had made more noise doing it than he'd bargained for.

"Damon was in the bathroom when he heard it," the woman said. "He grabbed a flashlight and rushed out there. He should have called the police instead."

Runyon agreed without saying so. He pushed the door open, stepped inside. Mrs. Henderson followed him and put on the lights. One car parked in there now, a silver Lexus that was probably her husband's; it had brand-new tires. The Mitsubishi wagon parked in the driveway would be hers.

He glanced around, getting the lay. Long cluttered workbench along this wall, the cartons of files in a triple-stacked row on the other side of the door. More cartons and gardening equipment along the far wall, three bicycles at the back end. Nothing disturbed or out of place that he could see.

He asked her, "Where was your husband when you found him?"

"There on the floor, next to his car."

"So he was attacked as soon as he opened the door and came inside."

"Yes. He hadn't taken more than three steps."

"Was his flashlight on?"

"When he came in, yes, but he was hit so quickly . . . he dropped it and it went out. He didn't see anything."

"How did the man leave? Same way he came in?"

"No, through one of the automatic doors. It was open."

"Overhead lights on when you came in?"

"Not until I put them on."

"Show me the button that works the garage door."

It was on the wall near the light switch. But not too near. Runyon pushed it, watched the door slide up quickly and with a moderate amount of noise. There was a light on the unit above the door, but it didn't come on. Broken? Looked that way.

The perp couldn't have been inside very long before Damon came blundering in. Just long enough to shine a flash beam around and break the door opener light. Why? There didn't seem to be any reason he'd want to leave that way, with the noise the unit made when it was activated, when he could slip out quietly in the dark the way he'd come in.

Samathana Henderson said, "My God . . . do you suppose he was in here *before* that night?"

"It's possible. Side door always kept locked?"

"At night, yes, but not always during the day. But he wouldn't . . . in broad daylight? Would he take that kind of risk?"

He might, if he was bold enough. Or crazy enough. The question, if he had been here before, was why take the risk? Hunting for something, maybe?

Runyon asked, "Have you looked through the garage since the attack? Checked to see if anything is missing?"

"Missing? I don't understand."

"Could you check now?"

"But . . . I can't imagine what . . ."

"Please, Mrs. Henderson. Just have a look around."

She spent fifteen minutes doing what he asked. Once she said, "I can't tell if any of Damon's business files are missing, you'd have to ask him." A little later she said, "As far as I can tell everything seems to be here," but two minutes later she contradicted herself.

Some boxes and a small trunk were jammed under a corner of the workbench. When she dragged the trunk out and opened it, she made a small, surprised sound. "Somebody's been in here."

Runyon went to peer over her shoulder. Photo albums, loose photos, loose letters, childhood drawings, other memorabilia.

"It was neatly arranged," she said. "The letters, the photos, all in packets. "Damon would never make a mess like this. Neither would Michael . . . my son, Michael. He'd have no reason to poke around in here."

"Some of those photos look fairly old."

"They are. Most of the things in here belonged to Damon's father. We brought the trunk over here after he died."

The father again. Runyon asked, "Can you tell if anything's been taken?"

"Not for sure. But . . . one or two of the albums, maybe . . . I seem to remember there were more than five. The letters and other stuff . . . I don't know. Damon should be able to tell you. Or Cliff."

"Do me a favor? Call Cliff tonight and ask him to come over, take a look, and then let me know what's missing."

"Yes, I'll do that."

"These letters. What type are they?"

"Oh, you know. Personal correspondence. From Lloyd to his wife when they were courting and when he was in the army in Korea. From the boys when they were away at camp."

"Same with the photos?"

"Yes. Snapshots and family portraits. Nothing . . . provocative. Nothing that would interest anyone outside the family. Why would the stalker steal letters and old photos? He couldn't have been *looking* for them. How could he know about the trunk? We've never told anybody we keep it in here."

Runyon was silent. He had no answers for her. Not even any guesses, at this point.

In the car he used his cell to call the agency. Tamara answered and he reported what he'd learned so far. She had nothing of interest to give him on the Henderson brothers and their families. He suggested that she shift the focus to Lloyd Henderson and his ex-wife, see if that avenue led anywhere.

"I'm on it," she said. "You through for the day up there?"

If he'd picked up any hot leads, even a warm lead, he'd have said no, he'd stay on it a while longer. If this had been a few months ago, before he met Bryn Darby and what lay ahead of him tonight was nothing more than four cold apartment walls, he'd have said the same thing. Push ahead, try to brace strangers in their homes, work as late as possible. But as things stood now . . .

"I'm through," he said. Until tomorrow morning, early. Tonight there was Bryn.

5

The pile owned by Gregory Pollexfen was typical of the homes in Sea Cliff, one of the city's wealthiest residential neighborhoods: imposing, ornately stylish, and probably worth upwards of five million even in the current real estate market. The architecture had a Spanish influence without actually being Spanish—a broad mix of beige stucco, red tile, wrought iron, and polished woodwork, with a variety of small trees and plants in huge terra-cotta urns on a balustraded front terrace, and gardens on both sides. Some ultraelitist types might not consider it among the premier houses along Sea Cliff Avenue; it loomed on the low inland hillside, rather than perched on the cliffs above China Beach on the seaward side. But to my jaundiced eye, it would do in a pinch.

A middle-aged, stoic-featured woman who was probably the housekeeper, though she wasn't outfitted that way, let me in and deposited me in a front parlor, all without uttering a word. I had just enough time to note that the undraped, floor-to-ceiling windows provided a sweeping view of the Golden Gate Bridge and the Marin headlands, and that the furnishings were expensive modern and the pictures on the walls all hunting and sporting scenes, before Pollexfen himself stumped in.

Stumped is the right word. He wasn't much older than me, but he moved in a slow, stiff, old man's way with the aid of a blackthorn cane, as if his joints pained him at every step. Arthritis, probably.

As we got the introductions out of the way, we sized each other up. He seemed to like what he saw; the faint smile he'd come in with widened a little and his eyes, steady on mine, reflected approval. As for me, I reserved judgment. You could see that once he'd been a powerful man, likely an athlete in his youth: an inch or so over six feet, thick-trunked and broad through the shoulders. Time and the afflictions that had invaded his body had taken their toll, as they do on all of us; his color wasn't good and his breathing had a little whistling catch in it. Still, he projected an aura of intensity and inner strength. His body may not be holding up well to the passing years, but I sensed that his mind was as sharp as ever. Those gray eyes radiated intelligence. Final analysis, based on first impression: a man who would make a staunch friend and a formidable enemy.

"I expect you'd like to see the library first thing," he said.

"Yes, I would."

"Follow me, then." The smile had faded; he was all

business now. "I was pleased to hear that we share the collecting gene. Fascinating hobby, isn't it, the acquisition of old books and magazines."

"And expensive, these days."

"Oh, yes. But I'm fortunate—the price of any given book or item of ephemera is not an issue with me. It's the rarity and availability. Certain titles have eluded me for years. They simply aren't available, no matter what one is willing to pay for them. Very frustrating. But then, the hunt is everything. If one could acquire everything one wanted, the game would lose some of its pleasure and excitement, don't you think?"

"I do, yes."

"Do you have much knowledge of antiquarian detective fiction?"

"A limited amount."

"But you do have an appreciation."

"If you're asking if I'll appreciate your collection, I'm sure I will."

"You may just be overwhelmed by it. My collection is one of the finest in the world." He said that without braggadocio. Just a proud statement of fact.

We went down a wide, tile-floored hallway, the ferrule tip of Pollexfen's cane making little hollow clicking sounds. Tile-inlaid archways opened at intervals into rooms on both sides. As we approached one of these near the end, I could hear another sound—the clicking of computer keys. Pollexfen turned in there, stepping aside to let me follow. Small office, a brunette in her midthirties ensconced behind a functional gray metal desk. Attractive, but severe-looking, as if she'd never found much to smile about in her life or work.

Pollexfen introduced us. Brenda Koehler, his secretary "and general factotum." She said through an impersonal smile, "I hope you're able to find out what happened to the missing books. The theft has everyone baffled." The words seemed impersonal, too, as if she didn't really care one way or the other.

"He has excellent credentials," Pollexfen said to her. "If anyone can get to the bottom of this, I'm sure he's the man."

She nodded. "I have the letter to Mr. Phillips ready for you to sign, Mr. Pollexfen."

"It can wait." He looked at me, said, "Business matter," and led me out into the hallway again. "Brenda's been with me for years. Handles my personal and household affairs. Indispensable."

"Which means she's also trustworthy."

"Absolutely. Even if she knew anything about antiquarian books, which she doesn't, she isn't permitted in the library alone."

"I understand none of the other members of your household is a bibliophile."

"That's right. Mrs. Jordan, the housekeeper, has been with me for years. Not even a reader and not overly bright, but above reproach. My wife's primary interest is in spending money on herself. My brother-in-law's hobby is making grandiose schemes and cheap women. If anyone in this house devised a way to steal those books, it's Jeremy Cullrane."

"Why do you say that?"

"We'll discuss it after you've seen the library."

At the end of the corridor was a set of double doors of some polished wood that might have been Philippine mahogany. Two locks, both deadbolts. Pollexfen used a key attached to a heavy silver ring to release the locks—the same key, I noticed, for both—and then reached inside to switch on the lights.

It was like walking into an exclusive bookshop, the kind that caters to well-heeled customers. Or a special exhibit in a library or museum. The room seemed to take up most of the back half of the house. It was thickly carpeted in some light blue weave; there were two overstuffed chairs with side tables, two floor lamps, an oak library table, a small desk, a gas-log fireplace with what looked to be an antique double-barreled shotgun mounted above it, and two sets of windows with heavy drapes in the back wall. The rest of it was books. Floor to ceiling on lacquered mahogany shelves. In stacks on the tables and here and there on the carpet. The upper shelves were reachable by one of those rolling library ladders strung on a brass rail that encircled the room.

Most of the volumes had bright dust jackets in Mylar protectors, the rest colorful bindings. That was my second impression of Pollexfen's library: color, much of it primary color. You were surrounded by it and the effect, enhanced by indirect ceiling light glinting off the Mylar, was almost dazzling.

Pollexfen was watching me and my reaction pleased him. He said, "Didn't I tell you, you might be overwhelmed?"

"You did and I am. Very impressive."

"Upwards of fifteen thousand volumes, catalogued and in alphabetical order. My primary interest is detective fiction of the last half of the nineteenth century and the first half of the twentieth. There is also a fair representation of post-1950 authors and titles, to the present day."

"All different types, I take it."

"Oh, yes. Sherlockiana. Whodunits, whydunits, howdunits. Hardboiled, police procedurals, spy novels, comic mysteries, category and mainstream thrillers—a sampling of every subgenre. Many are signed and inscribed. Six of those that were stolen are of that rarity."

"*The Maltese Falcon, Red Harvest, The Big Sleep, Fer-de-Lance, The Postman Always Rings Twice,* and *The Roman Hat Mystery*."

"Correct. Very good."

He led me to one section of shelves, pointed to a gap in the row of Hammett titles where the missing books had rested. "The *Falcon* is the most valuable because it was inscribed to a fellow *Black Mask* writer and mystery novelist, George Harmon Coxe. I'm sure you know his name."

I admitted that I'd read quite a few of Coxe's Flashgun Casey pulp stories.

"It's one of only two such association copies known," Pollexfen said, "the other being inscribed to another *Black Mask* writer, Frederick Nebel. I paid sixty thousand dollars for it twenty years ago. It's worth three to four times that amount in today's collecting market. One-of-a-kind volume."

Some of his collector's zeal gave way to melancholy as

he pointed out the empty places belonging to the Doyle, Christie, Stout, Cain, and Queen titles. "*Red Harvest, Roman Hat, Fer-de-Lance,* and *Postman* were inscribed to private individuals, so they're not quite as valuable as the *Falcon*. Nor are the Doyle and Christie. But all are high-five-figure items and virtually irreplaceable because of their rarity, the inscriptions and signatures, and the fact that they were all in near fine to fine condition. The 1892 Newnes first edition of *The Adventures of Sherlock Holmes* is the best copy any dealer or collector of my acquaintance has ever seen. As a collector yourself you can imagine how upset I was to find them missing."

"According to the insurance company report, you have no idea how they were taken or who took them."

His mouth quirked wryly. "A man I know suggested the Borrowers."

"The what?"

"Characters in a series of fantasy novels by Mary Norton. A secret race of tiny folk, descendants of the folkloric Little People, who 'borrow' things from humans. When something goes missing from inside your home and you can't figure out what happened to it, blame the Borrowers. That was Julian's smart-ass explanation."

"Who would Julian be?"

"Julian Iverson. A fellow bibliophile with a sometimes inappropriate sense of humor."

"You told him about the theft?"

"I needed a sympathetic ear, and there's none in this household."

"So you don't consider him a possible suspect?"

"Julian? My God, no. He's a collector, yes, but his tastes in literature differ greatly from mine. Fine bindings and children's books are his specialty. He has no interest in or knowledge of detective fiction."

"Would he know how valuable the missing titles are?"

"He would, but he's an old friend."

"Wealthy? Half a million dollars is a lot of money."

"His net worth is around four million," Pollexfen said. "Believe me, he's not the person responsible for this outrage."

"Have you told anyone else about the theft? Anyone outside this house?"

"Great Western, of course. My attorneys. A dozen or so other collectors and high-end booksellers—to alert them to be on the lookout for the missing titles. If anyone tries to sell the *Falcon* or any of the others to a reputable source, I'll be notified immediately."

"The operative word being 'reputable.' There must be collectors and sellers who'd buy prized items no questions asked."

"Too damn many," Pollexfen said. "That's my greatest fear. That one or all of these treasures will simply disappear into private hands."

"You mentioned your brother-in-law. Why do you think he might be responsible?"

"He has the scruples of a Washington lobbyist. Always in need of money for his schemes and his women and doesn't care how he gets it."

"What does he do for a living?"

Pollexfen laughed cynically. "He calls himself a promoter, but what he is, is a leech and a gigolo. He talks people into financing his get-rich-quick schemes. No doubt his various lady friends do the same behind their husbands' backs."

"But he doesn't get any from you."

"There was a time when I was foolish enough to fall for his line, but that time is long past."

"The two of you don't get along, then."

"Hardly. Jeremy can't stand me any more than I can stand him. He would steal the gold fillings out of my teeth if he thought he could get away with it."

"If that's the way it is, why do you let him live here?"

"Oh, I've come close to throwing him out half a dozen times. I would have, long ago, if it weren't for my wife."

"You mean she asked you not to?"

"On the contrary. She doesn't get along with Jeremy either."

"I don't understand."

"It's a complicated situation. You might say we feed off our dislike for one another."

That didn't sound too healthy to me. More to it than that? None of my business unless it had a bearing on my investigation, and too soon to press Pollexfen about it in any case.

I asked him, "Did you confront your brother-in-law about the theft?"

"If you mean did I accuse him, no, not without evidence. I did suggest that if I found out he was guilty, he would pay dearly for it. He laughed in my face."

"Does he know anything about rare books?"

"Very little, so far as I'm aware."

"Then how would he know which ones to steal? And where to sell them?"

"It wouldn't be difficult to find out. The Internet, booksellers, other collectors—the information is available to anyone who cares to do a little research."

I went across to the windows, drew the drapes aside on both. Barred. Sashes locked down tight.

"The drapes are always closed," Pollexfen offered. "Sunlight fades dust jacket backstrips. Even natural light will cause fading to some colors."

"I know. I have a similar arrangement in my home."

"Ah, yes. Pulp magazine spines fade, too, of course."

"I take it the door and windows are the only ways in and out of this room."

"Certainly. Were you thinking of secret panels or hidden nooks?"

"No. Asking questions, covering all the bases."

"Thorough man. I like that."

I went to examine the door locks. They were the kind that could be keyed from both sides, so Pollexfen could seal himself inside when he didn't want to be disturbed. No scratches or marks on them or anywhere on the door and jamb to indicate that they might have been forced.

As I started over to the desk, light reflecting off the barrels of the mounted shotgun caught my eye. Pollexfen took my upward glance as a sign of interest in the weapon. "A beauty, isn't it?" he said. "Nineteen twenty-six Parker GHE, twelve-gauge. Twenty-eight-inch uncut barrels, dual triggers, pistol grip stock, loads two-and-a-half-inch shells."

I didn't say anything. I'm not big on guns, even though—or maybe because—I own one and have had occasion to use it more than once.

"Inherited from my father," Pollexfen said. "We used to go hunting together—birds, mostly. Angelina and I did, too, when we were first married. She's a very good shot for a woman."

I had no comment on that, either.

"My only other hobby, hunting," he said. "Until a few years ago. Too old and arthritic now to tramp around the countryside."

Another pass. The hunter gene was left out of me; I like blood sports even less than guns. I gave my attention to the desk. Computer, telephone, a stack of what appeared to be auction catalogs, a pile of unused Mylar jacket protectors. The books stacked there, some with dust wrappers, some without, were apparently new acquisitions, awaiting shelving—not that there was much room left for them on any of the shelves.

"You do all the book buying yourself?" I asked.

"All the ordering, yes. Mainly from auction catalogs, a handful of antiquarian dealers, and through trades with other collectors. I used to haunt secondhand bookshops until the Internet put so many out of business."

"You handle the payments as well?"

"No, Brenda does that, unless a large bank transfer is necessary."

"So she has some knowledge of the collecting market."

"Some. But as I told you, she is completely trustworthy."

I did some more prowling, looking at the rows of

books. The shelves were all solid, the books on them loosely arranged so as to make for easy removal of any volume. I couldn't help looking at authors and titles along the way. Many more were familiar, including several who had contributed to pulp magazines as well as written novels: Leigh Brackett. Fredric Brown. Agatha Christie. John Dickson Carr. George Harmon Coxe. Norbert Davis. Erle Stanley Gardner. Ross Macdonald. John D. MacDonald. Frederick Nebel. Ellery Queen. Dorothy Sayers. Mickey Spillane. Rex Stout. Cornell Woolrich. Complete or near complete runs, evidently, of the works of these writers and hundreds more.

I asked, "Has anyone in this household, or any visitor, ever been in the library when you weren't here? For any reason?"

"No, never. I don't allow it."

"And you have the only key?"

"Yes. Which I keep in my possession at all times."

"Even while you sleep?"

"I put the key ring on my nightstand. And I'm a light sleeper. No one could have slipped in or out of the bedroom with it."

"While you shower or bathe, then."

"I'm never in the shower for more than five minutes."

"It doesn't take long to make a wax impression of a key."

"A possibility, I suppose," he conceded. "But that would leave a wax residue on the key, wouldn't it? I would have noticed."

"Not necessarily. The house alarm—who knows the code besides you?"

"My wife, her brother, Brenda, and the housekeeper."

"Written down anywhere?"

"No. I have it changed periodically, and I never forget anything as important as an alarm code."

"The alarm has never been breached?"

"Never."

"Then with all of that security and your precautions with the key, it doesn't seem possible anyone could have gotten in here, does it?"

Pollexfen's smile flickered back on, then off again. "The Holmesian dictum. If you eliminate the impossible, then whatever is left, no matter how improbable, must be the truth."

"So somebody must've found a way to use or duplicate your key."

"Or some other devilishly clever method. And not somebody, Jeremy Cullrane."

"There is one other explanation."

The smile flickered on and off again. "That I must have done it myself? Is that what you're thinking?"

"I'm not thinking anything yet, Mr. Pollexfen."

"I did not steal my own books," he said. "Why would I? What conceivable reason could I have?"

"There's the half million dollars' insurance."

"I don't need half a million dollars. I have more money than I can ever spend. Check into my finances, you'll find the absolute truth of that statement. I don't indulge in stocks or real estate or any other kind of speculation, I don't gamble, I don't have any of the usual vices. I collect vintage detective fiction. That's the one and only passion in life I have left. I'm the *last* person on earth who would spirit away eight of my most prized possessions, the cornerstones of a collection it has taken me forty years and quite a lot of money to assemble."

"So it would seem."

"I don't care about the insurance money," Pollexfen said. "I want my first editions back on the shelves where they belong. I wouldn't have filed the claim at all if the police had shown any real interest in finding them and my attorney hadn't insisted."

"What's your attorney's name?"

"Paul DiSantis. Wainright and Simmons."

I'd heard of the firm. High-powered corporate lawyers and ultrarespectable. "I'll want to talk to your wife, your brother-in-law, and your secretary."

"Certainly, but I suggest again, strongly, that you focus on Jeremy."

"Neither he nor your wife is here at the present, I take it."

"No. Jeremy spends little time under this roof, I'm happy to say, and Angelina is out indulging in one or more of her favorite activities. She should be back soon. Shopping tires her out, poor baby, and she likes to rest before going out on her evening rounds."

"Evening rounds?"

"Parties. She loves to party. I don't."

"Where can I find your brother-in-law?"

"Holding court at the Bayview Club downtown, or at his current lady friend's apartment." The emphasis he put on the word "lady" indicated he thought she was just the opposite. "A singer named Nicole Coyne. Brenda can give you her address."

"I'll talk to Brenda first, then. Alone, if you don't mind."

"Go right ahead." His mouth bent again at one corner. "You may have the dubious pleasure of meeting Angelina by the time you're done."

Dubious pleasure. Shopping always tires her out, poor baby. Out on her evening rounds. And he'd put the same emphasis on her name as he had on "lady," as if he considered it a misnomer and Angelina anything but angelic. He didn't seem to care for her any more than he did Jeremy Cullrane, had already removed her as beneficiary of his life insurance policy, and yet he continued to tolerate the marriage. The "we feed on our dislike for each other" statement must have included her, too.

Some household.

6

Brenda Koehler didn't have much to tell me. If she knew or suspected anything, she was keeping it to herself out of loyalty or fear of losing her job. Probably the latter; the whole time we talked in her office she kept glancing at the closed door, as if she thought her employer might be lurking and listening outside. Mostly she answered my questions with monosyllables.

The only real animation she showed was when I said, "Mr. Pollexfen seems to think his brother-in-law is responsible for the thefts." She sat up straighter in her chair and a little color came into her pale cheeks. Her tongue flicked over her thin upper lip before she responded.

"That's not possible," she said.

"What makes you so sure?"

"Jeremy . . . Mr. Cullrane is not that kind of man, not a thief."

"Your employer believes he is."

"They don't get along," she said stiffly. "Mr. Pollexfen . . . well, he's always ready to believe the worst about Jeremy."

"Why is that? Why don't they get along?"

"I don't know. It's none of my business."

"Do they argue often?"

"I . . . can't say. Mr. Cullrane isn't here very much during my working hours."

"Money seems to be an issue between them," I said. "A leech, Mr. Pollexfen called him."

"That's not true. He doesn't take money from Mr. Pollexfen."

"How do you know he doesn't?"

"Part of my job is to pay the household expenses."

"And you've never written any checks to Mr. Cullrane?"

"No. Never. He has a very good job. He doesn't need to be supported."

"Some kind of promoter, isn't he?"

"Music. He books performers for small clubs and charity events."

"Sounds like you know him fairly well."

"Why do you say that?" Defensive now.

"So you don't know him well."

"No. I . . . no."

More color in her cheeks, almost a flush. Maybe she didn't know him well, but she'd like to.

"I understand he's quite a ladies' man," I said.

". . . Did Mr. Pollexfen tell you that? It's not true."

"No?"

"He has a . . . steady relationship. He's not interested in other women."

Meaning she'd made her feelings known to him in one way or another and the attraction wasn't mutual. I said, "Nicole Coyne."

"What?"

"The woman he has the steady relationship with. Nicole Coyne."

"Oh. Yes."

"I understand you have her address. Why is that?"

"Mr. Cullrane gave it to me. In case someone calls for him."

"Does he receive many calls?"

"Here? No."

"The calls he does receive. From anyone in particular?"

"It's not my place to give out that information. You'll have to ask him."

"I take it he spends a lot of his time with Ms. Coyne?"

"Yes." Tight-lipped.

I asked for the address. She gave it to me, along with the singer's phone number. I wasn't going to get any more out of her about Jeremy Cullrane, so I moved on to a different subject.

"What can you tell me about Mrs. Pollexfen?"

She stiffened again. "Tell you? I don't know what you mean."

"Do you think it's possible she had anything to do with the theft?"

"I . . . don't know."

"Eliminate Mr. Pollexfen and Mr. Cullrane, and yourself and the housekeeper, and Mrs. Pollexfen is the only one left."

"Yes. That's true."

"So you do think she could be involved."

"I didn't say that. Please don't put words in my mouth."

"Are the two of you on friendly terms?"

"Friendly? I hardly know the woman."

"That's right, she's not here much during the day, is she?"

"Not much, no."

"Spends most of her time shopping."

"Shopping," Brenda Koehler said.

She didn't put any emphasis on the word, but it came out through lips pinched even more tightly; I had the impression of disapproval and scorn. As if she knew or had her suspicions that Angelina Pollexfen spent her days doing something more than spending her husband's money.

"Does she have other outside interests?" I asked.

"I'm sure I don't know."

"What about money? Her husband give her carte blanche or put limits on her spending?"

"She has credit cards. Several."

"Uses them all regularly, does she?"

"I can't tell you that without Mr. Pollexfen's permission."

"Run up any large debts?"

The thin lips pinched again. But all she said was, "Please don't ask me any more questions about financial matters. I don't have the authority to answer them."

I'd run out of questions, period. Trying to extract specific information from Brenda Koehler in these surroundings was pretty much a wasted effort. The perfect discreet employee. But insecure nonetheless; she'd continued to glance at the closed door every third or fourth question the entire time we'd been talking.

I put an end to the interview, left her, and went out to the front parlor where Pollexfen had said he'd be waiting. He was sitting in an armchair reading one of his mystery books the way I read my pulps—carefully, with it open only about a third of the way so as not to strain the binding. When I came in, he bookmarked his place and hoisted himself, wincing, to his feet.

"Damn arthritis," he said. "Hell to grow old, isn't it?"

"Better than the alternative."

"Trite but true. Did Brenda have anything illuminating to tell you?"

"Not really."

"I didn't think she would. My wife still isn't home. You're welcome to wait, if you like."

"No, thanks. Another time."

"Come back tomorrow morning. I'll make sure she's here."

"Thanks, but I'd prefer to talk to her somewhere else. Your brother-in-law as well. You have no objections?"

"Of course not. Suppose I arrange for you to have lunch with Angelina?"

"Lunch isn't necessary."

"She'll be downtown anyway. As usual. And one has to eat."

"All right, then. If she's agreeable."

"She will be," Pollexfen said. "As for Jeremy, you'll have to make your own arrangements." He added meaningly, "If you can catch him."

It was four thirty when I drove away from Sea Cliff. Tamara would still be at the agency, but I didn't feel like fighting crosstown traffic. Easier to phone her, then take the shorter route home through the park and on up to Diamond Heights.

When I reached the Palace of the Legion of Honor I pulled over into the main parking lot to make the call. The Henderson case first—I asked Tamara if Jake had checked in yet.

"Few minutes ago," she said. "He thinks the stalker's motive might have something to do with the father, Lloyd Henderson."

"Because of the grave desecration?"

"Yep. Only problem with that is, the man's been dead five years. Doesn't seem likely somebody'd all of a sudden decide to go after his sons."

"You look into the father's background yet?"

"Doing that now. Another model citizen. Dentist. Retired four years before he died. What could a dentist've done that'd make some dude start slinging acid?"

"Fillings gone bad, maybe."

She laughed. "Hey, who says you don't have a sense of humor. Every now and then you get off a funny line."

"By accident, no doubt." I went on to fill her in on the interview with Gregory Pollexfen.

She said, "Rich people," in her scornful way. "So what's your take? Man swipe his own books?"

"Possible, but it seems to be another case of no motive. Unless you've come up with facts I don't know about yet."

"Nope. Rivera was right—Pollexfen's a financial rock. Got more money than you or I will ever see."

"How about the others in the ménage?"

"Well, Jeremy Cullrane's no angel. Been in trouble before."

"What kind of trouble?"

"Assault case a few years ago—argument with the husband of a woman he was shagging that led to a brawl. Husband pressed charges but dropped them later. One other mark on Cullrane's record: arrest five years ago for aggravated assault, charges dropped for lack of evidence."

"A sweetheart."

"Yeah. And a loser. Considers himself a player, but he doesn't play real well. Reputed to've dropped a bundle in a deal that went sour five years ago, right before the assault arrest."

"What kind of deal?"

"Details a little hazy, but I'll find out."

"His own money?"

"Not unless he's been dealing drugs on the side."

"Could be Pollexfen's. Through his sister."

"Well, the Cullranes grew up lower middle class in Fresno, so no financial resources there. With his business record, doesn't seem too likely he'd have friends or connections for big-bucks loans."

"Promoter, right? Booking agent for club acts?"

"Among other things," Tamara said.

"Where's his office?"

"Doesn't have one. There's a listing—Jeremy Cullrane Associates, on Geary. But it's just a mail drop—I checked."

"Any hint what he might be involved in now? Some kind of deal, say, that would require a large sum of cash?"

"Not so far."

"He's seeing a singer named Nicole Coyne, lives in North Beach." I spelled the name and recited the address. "See what you can find out about her and her financial situation."

"Will do."

"Anything I ought to know about Mrs. Pollexfen?"

"Well, she's a boozer. Two DUI arrests, lost her license for six months on the second. EMT call to their house three years ago—toxic reaction to prescription drugs and alcohol that put her in the hospital for three days."

"What did she do before she hooked up with her husband?"

"Travel agent. She's more than thirty years younger than him. True love at first sight, you think?"

"On his part, maybe," I said. "I'd like to know if there was a prenup."

"I'll see if I can find out."

"How faithful she's been, too. Any whisper stuff, links with prominent men. Both Pollexfen and his secretary made sly little remarks about her daily 'shopping trips.' If she has been cheating, she couldn't have been very discreet about it."

"Oh boy," Tamara said, "down and dirty."

"One more thing. Any expensive habits or vices—her, and also her brother and husband."

"Poor Tamara. Work, work, work."

"You know you love it," I said.

"Well, I've got the energy for it now. Sure is amazing what getting laid can do for a girl's stamina."

Kerry said, "I have news."

There was a time, less than a year ago, when she'd made that same announcement, and the news had been bad enough to knock my world off its axis. Breast cancer. But long, difficult weeks of radiation therapy had done its job; she'd been cancer-free for several months now, as of her most recent checkup two weeks ago. This news couldn't be linked to the disease. She was smiling and her green eyes were aglow.

"Good news, right?"

"Very good. Get yourself a beer and me a glass of wine and I'll tell you." When I'd done that and we had drinks in hand, she said, "You are looking at Bates and Carpenter's newest vice president."

"Hey! A promotion!"

"Effective immediately. Bigger office, bigger perks, and a bigger paycheck every month. How about that?"

"Terrific." We clinked glasses. "More hours, too, though, I'll bet."

"Probably. Do you mind?"

"Not if you're up to it."

"I'm up to it. Jim Carpenter thinks so, too, or he wouldn't have offered the promotion."

"The important thing is what your oncologist thinks. I don't have to remind you what he said about too much stress. . . ."

"No, you don't. I know my limitations, don't worry."

"It's my nature to worry, especially where you're concerned."

She patted my cheek and leaned up to kiss me. "You're sweet," she said. Then she said, "You're staring at me again."

"Am I?"

"I catch you doing that a lot lately. I must really look different, huh?"

"Beautiful. Gorgeous."

"Ten years younger?" she asked, pleased.

"At least."

She'd had a face-lift a few weeks ago. Her treat to herself after the breast cancer ordeal. I'd been leery of it at first, all that slicing and dicing, and when I first saw her after the surgery, all bandaged and bruised and swollen like the victim of a bad accident, I'd been more than a little anxious. (Not Emily, though; nothing much bothered that kid of ours anymore.) Kerry had spent two and a half weeks holed up in the condo, going out only for post-op visits to her plastic surgeon, doing her ad agency work by home computer as she had during the cancer radiation treatments. When the last of the bandages came off and the scars finally healed, good-bye, anxiety, hello, happy surprise. The minor age wrinkles and eye bags and mouth lines that had bothered her, if not me, were gone and she truly did look ten years younger. More beautiful than ever. No wonder I kept staring at her.

"Where's Emily?" I asked.

"It's her choral group night, remember?"

"That's right. Our daughter, the budding chanteuse. So how about you and I celebrate the promotion?"

"What did you have in mind?"

"Oh, something Tamara told me this afternoon, about stamina."

"And that is?"

I told her. Then I told her, juicily, what I had in mind. She actually blushed a little.

Face-lifts do wonders, all right. For a woman's self-image and morale. And for a man's libido.

7

JAKE RUNYON

He picked Bryn up at six thirty. She was ready; she never kept him waiting. The scarf covering the frozen left side of her face was midnight blue with some kind of gold design. When he'd first met her four months ago, she wore dark-colored or paisley scarves with her plain sweaters, skirts, slacks. The outfits were still the same, but now the scarves had color in them. Her way of dressing up for him.

Subdued tonight. She had periodic bouts of depression, she'd told him, and when she was depressed she was even quieter than usual. "I'm not very hungry," she said. "Do you mind if we drive for a while before we eat?"

"Where would you like to go?"

"I don't care. Anywhere."

"Down the coast? Highway One?"

"Yes, all right."

He'd told her that he liked to drive, even on those days when the job required him to log in a lot of miles. She understood his restlessness, his need not to be trapped by stationary walls. She preferred the confines of her brown-shingled house—familiar, the place where she'd been happy before the stroke that had left her with partial facial paresis. But sometimes a restlessness seized her, too. At night, for the most part. Days, she had her watercolors and charcoal sketches and the graphics design business she was trying to build up.

He was seeing her three or four times a week now. Mostly at night, even on weekends. She didn't like to go out much in the daylight hours. They had dinner usually, at one of the same two coffee shops on Taraval. In other restaurants, places where she wasn't known, people had a tendency to stare at her or to cluck their stupid tongues because of the scarf and the way she was forced to eat, twisting open the good side of her mouth to take the food, chewing and swallowing in awkward movements with her head down over her plate because no matter how careful she was, pieces of food or dribbles of liquid sometimes leaked out. If there was one thing she hated more than anything else, it was pity—a stranger's pity worst of all.

Now and then they took in a movie; she was comfortable in darkened theaters. In good weather they went for walks on Ocean Beach or Land's End, away from people. Or sat in the car somewhere and talked. He'd been inside the brown-shingled house only twice, once to see her paintings and graphic designs, once for a glass of wine.

He had not touched her except to take her arm when they went up or down stairs, or to help her on and off with her coat. And yet a closeness had developed between them, a slow-developing bond of trust. Different by far from his relationships with the other two women in his life, the caretaker role he'd had to assume with half-crazy, alcoholic Andrea, the fire and passion and soul-deep love he'd shared with Colleen. If it ever moved to another level with Bryn . . . all right. Now, what they had was enough. They'd never discussed it, but he thought she felt the same way.

Most people would find their relationship odd, he supposed. If he'd had to explain it to somebody else, he couldn't have found the right words. The closest he could come was that before they met, they'd been like a couple of turtles hiding in their shells. Hers fashioned by the stroke and a shit of a husband who couldn't deal with her affliction and losing custody of her nine-year-old son to his father; his made from the loss of Colleen and the six months death watch he'd had to endure while the cancer ate at her from within. Now the turtles' heads were out, only partway but still out. A couple of lonely, damaged creatures, blinking in the light, finding understanding and acceptance in each other and taking solace from it.

He drove them down through Pacifica, over Devil's Slide, to Half Moon Bay. Nice night, clear, the stars cold and nail-head bright in a black sky. Bryn had very little to say, focused inward. He didn't try to make conversation. The silences between them were comfortable now.

At one of the stoplights in Half Moon Bay he said, "Go on a little farther, or head back?"

"A little farther."

She didn't speak again until they were approaching the beach at San Gregorio. Then, "I saw my doctor today."

"What did he say?"

"No change. He's honest, he doesn't give out false hope. It's almost certain now that I'll have the paralysis for the rest of my life."

"He could still be wrong."

"He's not wrong. Sometimes . . ."

When she didn't go on right away, Runyon glanced over at her. She was staring straight ahead, back stiff, knees together, hands cupped together in her lap—the sitting posture of a young girl.

"Sometimes," she said finally, "I feel like I'm going crazy."

"I know the feeling." Mourning Colleen in the all-consuming way he had, Joshua lost to him, work his only sanctuary . . . he'd been close to the edge himself, closer than he'd let himself believe. "But you won't let it happen."

"Won't I? I still have nights when I just want to . . . give up."

"I know how that is, too."

"No, I mean . . ."

"I know what you mean."

"Did you ever feel that way? After your wife died?"

"Yes."

"Ever . . . you know, come close to ending it all?"

"A couple of times."

"How close?"

"Close enough." He wouldn't give her the details— metallic taste of the .357 Magnum muzzle in his mouth, finger tight on the trigger, sweat pouring off him, the sudden fevered shaking that once made him drop the gun into his lap. No, that was a piece of his own private hell he'd never share with anyone.

"What stopped you?" she asked.

"I wanted to live more than I wanted to die."

"I . . . I'm not sure I feel the same way."

"If you didn't, you wouldn't be here."

"That's not necessarily true. I think I'm a coward."

"You're not a coward," he said. "Cowards go through with it, leave the mess for somebody else to clean up."

"I wouldn't do it that way, the bloody way."

"There're other kinds of messes. The people you leave behind. You wouldn't do that to your son, would you? Leave him that kind of legacy?"

She made a soft, anguished sound. "Oh, God. Bobby."

"No," he said, "you wouldn't."

"I miss him," she said, "I miss him so much. Two weekends a month . . . it's so damn unfair."

Her visitation privileges, she meant. The ex-husband was a lawyer, the self-righteous, conniving type. He'd not only found a self-serving excuse to abandon Bryn when he learned her paralysis was likely to be permanent, he'd sued for custody of the boy and convinced a sympathetic judge to rule in his favor. He had another woman now; Bryn thought he might've had her even before the stroke. The plan was for the boy to have a stepmother sometime this summer.

Runyon had met Robert Jr. once, on one of Bryn's weekends with him last month. Nice kid, nine years old;

smart, shy, liked computers and video games and football. No question that he loved his mother, but he seemed a little uneasy around her. Wouldn't look at her directly, as if the covered half of her face frightened him or made him nervous.

Runyon said, "You'll have more time with him as he gets older."

"Will I? You didn't have any time with your son."

"Different situation. My first wife was a vindictive alcoholic—I think I told you that. She poisoned Joshua against me. After twenty years, there's no antidote. Don't let your ex do that to Bobby."

"He hasn't. I don't think he will. Robert can be a prick, but he cares about Bobby. And doesn't care enough about me to hurt me any more than he already has."

"What about the new woman he's with?"

"I've never met her and I'm not sure I want to."

"Know much about her?"

"No, except that she sells real estate. She's been good to Bobby—he likes her."

"Can I ask you a personal question?"

"Yes."

"Have you talked to Bobby about the paralysis?"

"Mother to son? Yes, as much as you can to a nine-year-old about a thing like that."

"Let him see your face, without the scarf?"

Nothing for a few seconds. Then, "No."

"Might help him understand better."

"It would be cruel to subject him to that. He's just a child."

"Afraid of his reaction?"

"I don't . . . What do you mean?"

"That he won't be able to deal with it. Pull away from you."

"You've seen my face," she said. "Half a Halloween mask."

Runyon had seen it only once, the first time their lives intersected, when he'd chased away a couple of smart-ass kids after one of them yanked off her scarf in a Safeway parking lot. Dim light, but it hadn't seemed so bad to him. He said, "Eye of the beholder. It didn't scare me away."

"You're an adult."

"And you're Bobby's mother. He needs you."

"And he can have me," she said bitterly, "two weekends every month."

"I only saw you together once, but you were tentative around him."

"What the hell does that mean? Tentative?"

"No hugs, no kisses. You didn't even touch him."

"Oh, for God's sake. That's not true."

"It's true, Bryn. I wouldn't lie to you."

"You're a fine one to dispense parental advice. How many times did you hug *your* son when he was growing up?"

"I didn't have a choice. You do."

"That's enough! I don't like being told how to deal with my son!"

He'd pushed it too hard, made her angry. A fine one to dispense parental advice.

"All right," he said, "I'm sorry."

"You should be."

"I was out of line. I won't do it again."

"Better not if you want to keep this friendship."

Quiet again until they were approaching Devil's Slide on the way back. But she'd been thinking about his perceptions, weighing them; she broke the silence by saying, "Jake? About what you said earlier . . ."

"I didn't mean to upset you."

"Just being honest—I know. You were right, I don't touch Bobby. I'm afraid to touch him, afraid he'll draw away from me. He's all I have left. I couldn't stand to lose him, too."

"You won't."

"It's just so hard," she said. "So hard."

"Don't let him feel you're rejecting him and he won't reject you. I think I'm right about that. Loving close is always better than loving at a distance."

It was after nine by the time they got back to the city. The coffee shop at Taraval and Nineteenth Avenue stayed open until midnight; they had dinner there, in a rear booth. A stranger sitting across from them couldn't keep his fat eyes off Bryn. The third time he glanced over, Runyon caught his gaze and held it, impaled him until the man shifted both his gaze and his body and kept his attention on his plate, where it belonged. Damn people, anyway.

He took Bryn home afterward, walked her to the door. Before she unlocked it and went in, she said, "Thank you."

"For what?"

"Putting up with me. Being honest. I'm such a screwed-up mess."

"Not any more than me and a whole lot of others."

"I almost cancelled tonight. So depressed after I saw the doctor."

"I'm glad you didn't."

"So am I."

"Better now?"

"Better," she said. "What you said, about Bobby, about loving close . . . it makes sense."

"When can we get together again?"

"Not tomorrow. My mother's night to call."

Her mother lived in Denver, she'd told him, and was the only other person she could talk to about personal issues. But only for short periods; the mother tended to become weepy and critical.

"Wednesday, then?"

"Yes, Wednesday. Good night, Jake."

"Good night."

It was a short drive from Moraga Street to his apartment building on Ortega. On the way he turned his cell phone back on. He'd taken to switching it off when he was with Bryn; urgent calls were a rarity in the evening and their time together had become too important to let routine business intrude.

One voice-mail message, from Cliff Henderson in Los Alegres: "I looked through the trunk in Damon's garage like you asked. The only thing missing I'm sure about is one of the photo albums. Mostly old pictures taken on hunting and fishing trips—Damon and me, my father, some of his hunting buddies. No damn idea why that crazy bugger would steal it."

Too late to call Henderson back now. He'd talk to him about the missing album in the morning, in person.

Coming in late to the apartment, facing the emptiness, wasn't so bad on the nights he was with Bryn. He turned on the TV for noise, booted up his laptop to check his e-mail. All he ever got were occasional business messages and spam, but he always checked it before he went to bed. One e-mail from Tamara tonight, sent after five o'clock, with some more background information on the Henderson brothers, their father, and their remarried mother. Didn't seem to be much there, but you never knew what might prove to be important until you got deeper into an investigation.

In the bedroom later, he sat on the edge of the bed and looked at the framed portrait of Colleen on the night-stand. Another nightly ritual, but that, too, was different than it had been before. She would've liked Bryn, approved of him seeing her. Encouraged it, even. Just one of the things he'd loved about Colleen: she'd always wanted what was best for him.

8

SCHEMER

He sat on the edge of the motel tub, burning the last of the Henderson snapshots.

The cracked, leather-bound album lay spread open on his lap. The door was closed, the rattling fan switched on to clear away the smoke and keep it from setting off the smoke alarm. There were only a handful of snaps left in the album. He'd burned the rest over the past several days, a few each day.

He removed one of the last from its plastic sleeve, looked at it for a time. Lousy, like all of them. Poor composition, bad use of light and background. Cheap camera, probably. Amateur shit. He turned it over to read what was written on the back—"Hayden and George, Aug 1998"—and then spun the wheel of his lighter and touched the flame to one corner. It burned slow at first, then fast. When the heat began to sear his fingers, he dropped the charred remains into the toilet with the others.

Unexpected find, this album. He hadn't been looking for anything like it, anything at all the afternoon he'd slipped into Damon Henderson's garage. Bold move, going in there in broad daylight. Proof that he could breach their lives any time and any place he wanted to, that he owned them now whether they knew it yet or not. No real risk involved. Getting into the garage had been ridiculously easy. Wear a khaki shirt, carry a flashlight and a clipboard, wear a badge that looks authentic, act like you belong in the neighborhood, and people take you for a meter reader or a workman and pay no real attention to you.

Sifting through all those boxes and then finding the trunk with the albums in it—that had been almost as much of a rush as Sunday night's visit. Bad few seconds when Henderson came blundering in, spoiling the planned acid bath for his CPA records and his car, but the rest of it had turned out real well. Hitting him with the tire iron, straddling him, whispering to him, hitting him again and hearing him scream . . . oh, yeah! He'd had to fight himself not to use the tire iron a third time, split Henderson's skull wide open, but it wasn't the right place or the right time. Henderson wouldn't have suffered enough. And there hadn't been enough time to tell him why he was suffering. That would come later.

He looked at and burned two more photos, taking his time. The last one was in color, a posed shot, poorly centered and badly filtered so that the background was muzzy and the images not sharp. But they were clear enough for identification, even without what was written on the back: "Cliff, Damon, and Dad, Oct 2000." He lifted the snapshot close to his mouth and spat on each of the images before he set it on fire. Held it longer than any of the others, watching it burn, savoring the blackened destruction of the images until the flame reached his fingers and made him let go. Some of the ashes missed the toilet bowl. He scraped them into his hand, brushed them in.

Then he stood, unzipped his fly, urinated onto the ashes.

Spat one last time on the yellow-black mess and flushed it away.

At the sink he washed his hands. They still felt unclean when he was done, so he washed them again. Better. He used the towel, making sure his palms and wrists were completely dry. Then he switched off the fan and went out into the main room.

Typical cheap motel room, designed for anonymity. The perfect hideout. He smiled at the thought of "hideout" and sat down on the lumpy bed.

The spiral-bound notebook was in his briefcase, along with the five-by-seven color portrait and the digital snapshots he'd taken at the cemetery. He unlocked the case, took them out, lay back with his head propped against the headboard. He looked at the portrait first, looked at it for a long time. Familiar face, but clouded by time—a kid's memory. But he'd gotten to know it well from the portrait, as well as he ever would. Each time he looked at it he felt a great tenderness well up inside. She'd been so pretty. Not the plastic, Hollywood kind of prettiness—genuine, the girl-next-door kind. High cheekbones, small nose, small cleft in the well-shaped chin. And not just attractive outside, but good inside. You could see the goodness shining in those soft brown eyes.

After a time he put the portrait down and again read the last few notebook pages, shaping each sentence with his lips, lingering over the important passages. Sad, bitter, painful. Full of love and sorrow and desperation. Full of pleading—a tacit plea to him, now, because there was nobody else.

Testimony.

Damning testimony.

Wet filled his eyes. He used a clean edge of the pillow-case to dry them, then returned the notebook and the portrait to his briefcase. The rage was in him again, strong and driving. It made the blood beat loud in his temples.

Another face popped out of his memory—thin, wrinkled, not pretty at all. "Damn you," he said aloud, "why didn't you read what she wrote? Didn't you suspect, didn't you care? And why didn't you give me the notebook while that son of a bitch was still alive? *He'd* have been the one to suffer then. I'd have made him suffer!"

He lay still for a time until his pulse rate slowed and the rage started to fade. No use blaming her. She'd only done what she believed was right for him. But she shouldn't have waited, shouldn't have let him find out the way he had, so long afterward, when it was too late.

He picked up the cemetery photos, shuffled through them. Not too bad. Decent composition considering the darkness and the digital camera. The urn, the ashes, the monument . . . all clearly defined. The vapors from the acid made a neat wavy pattern on the one of the headstone. Mementos he could enjoy for years to come.

The anger was gone now, but his eyes had begun to sting. The pillowcase hadn't been properly laundered after all. His face, his hands . . . itchy, dirty. He hurried into the bathroom, stripped off his clothes, and stood under a scalding hot shower to make himself clean again.

9

JAKE RUNYON

The Henderson Construction Company was building three new homes in a hillside cul-de-sac on Los Alegres' southwestern edge. Two homes framed out and in different stages of completion, the third staked and ready for the concrete foundation to be poured. All three sites were fenced—new Cyclone fencing, from the look of it, probably put up after the vandalism. The gates were open now, half a dozen pickups parked inside, a forklift unloading board lumber from a flatbed truck on one site, a dozen or so workmen making the usual amount of noise.

Runyon left his Ford outside on the street and hunted up Cliff Henderson at the the home nearest completion. They went over by a large, portable tool-storage shed to talk. Even before Henderson pointed it out, Runyon had noticed the acid damage done to the unit's metal siding.

"Bastard couldn't get inside the shed," Henderson said. "Didn't have enough time to burn the locks off, so he just splashed acid on the sides. If he had gotten in . . . thousands of dollars' worth of tools down the toilet."

"No attempt at a second pass?"

"If he was thinking about it, the fencing, police patrols, a private security patrol I hired changed his mind. I can't afford to take any more losses on these sites."

"How's your brother?"

"Better. Might let him go home today, tomorrow for sure."

"You have a chance to talk to him about the missing photo album?"

"On the phone last night. He can't figure it either. Why the guy would risk poking around in Damon's garage during the day, why he took the album. Just gets crazier and crazier."

"Mostly photos of the two of you and your father, you said."

"Yeah. On the fishing and hunting trips we used to take."

"Any particular place?"

"Same place every time. Hunting camp in Mendocino County, east of Fort Bragg. Dad built it back in the fifties."

"Still own the property?"

"Sure. Damon and I don't get up there as much as we used to, but two of Dad's old hunting buddies still go now and then. They don't hunt anymore, they're both in their seventies, but they fish and play cribbage . . . you know, just to get away for a few days."

"Hayden Brock one of them?"

"That's right. And Dr. George . . . George Thanopolous."

Runyon asked, "Anything unusual happen on any of the trips?"

"Like what?"

"Anything at all. Anything that might have been in those snapshots."

"Not on the trips Damon and me were on. We caught fish, shot a buck if we were lucky, played cards, drank beer, told stories, goofed around. Guy stuff, that's all."

"How about on the ones your father took with his buddies?"

"Not that I know about." Henderson frowned. "What're you getting at? This stalking crap couldn't have any connection to my dad or the camp."

"Then why was the album stolen?"

"Christ, I don't know. But Dad . . . he was salt of the earth. Ask anybody, they'll tell you. He's been gone five years. And the last time he was up at the camp was three or four years before that, before he got sick. You're barking up the wrong tree."

Runyon spent the rest of the morning making the rounds of friends, neighbors, and business acquaintances of the Henderson brothers. None of them had anything to tell him. The Hendersons were great guys, good family men, regular churchgoers. Honest as the day is long. No harm in either of them. Incredible that anybody could hate them enough to do what had been done to them.

By the time he finished, he was convinced that the motive for the harrassment and assault lay elsewhere. Something to do with the father?

Wrong tree or not, it was worth some more barking.

Hayden Brock leaned back in the swivel chair in his law office, hooked his thumbs under the straps of his old-fashioned galluses, and gave Runyon an unreadable lawyer stare. His eyes were a cold blue under bushy white eyebrows. White hair, fine as rabbit fur, and a thick white mustache gave him a stern and frosty look.

"If you're looking for dirt on Lloyd Henderson," he said flatly, "you won't find it here."

Runyon said, "The only thing I'm looking for is answers to why his sons are being stalked."

"Terrible thing, that, but it doesn't have anything to do with Lloyd."

"Everybody keeps telling me that."

"But you don't seem to listen."

"When you can't find an answer in one place, you look in another. Right now I'm looking at Lloyd Henderson."

"Just because the first act of vandalism was the desecration of his grave?"

"That's one reason. Another is the stolen photo album. Can you offer any explanation for that?"

"No."

"Do you know of anything unusual that happened on the family's hunting and fishing trips to Mendocino County?"

"I do not."

"On any of the trips that didn't include the two sons?"

"No. Weekend getaways, that's all they were."

"Men only? No women allowed?"

The white mustache bristled. "What kind of question is that?"

"A simple one."

"Our wives didn't share our passion for the outdoors."

Lawyerspeak. Factual but evasive. Runyon said, "So there were no women in the photos that were stolen."

"I just told you our wives never went along, didn't I?"

Same evasive response. "What about after Lloyd's divorce?"

"Now what are you asking?"

"He didn't remarry. I assume he had women friends over the last twenty years of his life. Did he ever take one of them to the hunting camp?"

"No."

"Was he involved with any particular woman after his divorce?"

"If he was, it's none of your business."

"You won't give me a name?"

"I will not. Why should I?"

"The more people I can talk to . . ."

"People who know Cliff and Damon, yes. Not those who knew Lloyd." Brock leaned forward so abruptly his chair back made a sharp cracking noise. "I suggest you concentrate on finding the link between the two sons and the maniac responsible for harassing them. You won't find it with their father."

"If you say so, Mr. Brock."

"I do say so. Now suppose you get on with your business so I can proceed with mine."

End of interview. Runyon stood up.

"Just remember what I said about looking for dirt," Brock said. "It won't get you anywhere you need to go."

Second time Brock had used the phrase "looking for dirt." Protesting too much. If there was no dirt to dig up, why keep mentioning it?

George Thanopolous lived in a large ranch-style home on three or four acres atop one of the west-side hills. The elderly woman who answered the door identified herself as Mrs. Thanopolous, and when Runyon told her who he was and why he was there, she said, "It's awful, isn't it? Just awful. Those poor boys. But there isn't anything George or I can tell you. If we knew anything that might help, we would have told the police."

"I'm sure you would have. But I'd still like to talk to your husband. Is he home?"

"Out back with his bees."

"Bees?"

"His hobby, you know. Beekeeping and making honey. Just go on around the side of the house and across the terrace. You'll see the apiary and bee house from there."

Runyon followed her instructions. The terrace was broad and flagstoned, with a sweeping view of the town spread out below, part of the valley and the bordering hills to the east. Beyond the terrace was a wide grassy field sprinkled here and there with low white boxes that must be the beehives. Nobody was working among them except bees.

A flagstone path led through the field above the hives, to a shedlike building painted the same bright white. The door was open, and as Runyon approached he heard a hammer banging away inside and then spotted the man using it. He stopped outside and called, "Dr. Thanopolous?"

George Thanopolous was well up in his seventies, his face mostly free of wrinkles—small, energetic, bright-eyed. He didn't seem to mind having a stranger turn up unexpectedly at his bee house. Particularly a stranger with Runyon's credentials and purpose.

The drop-lit interior was cramped and crowded. Workbench, shelves, Peg-Boards of tools and beekeeping equipment—bee veils, smokers, elbow-length gloves, strips of lathe, glue pots, brushes, a bunch of other items Runyon didn't recognize. The place had a faint odor, partly sweet like melons and partly sour like decaying flesh. Bee venom? Probably. It sure wasn't clover honey.

Thanopolous indicated the wood strips that he'd been nailing together into a frame. "Don't mind if I finish making this comb while we talk? Good. Want to get a few more done today. Stool over there if you care to sit down, just move the bee escapes to the bench here."

"I'll stand, thanks."

"Suit yourself." Thanopolous drove another nail with his tack hammer. "Don't know what I can tell you," he said. "Cliff and Damon are both good boys, but Ellen and I don't see much of them anymore. Why anybody'd want to stalk them . . . don't have a clue."

"Both family men. Faithful husbands, honest in their business practices."

"Absolutely. Their father was strict with them, growing up. Single parent, you know."

"Yes. There doesn't seem to be anything in their lives that triggered the attacks. I'm looking into the possibility that the motive may have something to do with Lloyd Henderson."

"Lloyd? Oh, now, that's not possible. He passed away some years ago."

"I know. But the first act was the desecration of his grave."

"True. That struck me, too. Just so damn senseless."

"You and Lloyd Henderson were close friends?"

"That's right. Thirty years . . . no, thirty-five."

"Went hunting and fishing together regularly."

"Up to his camp in the mountains. With his boys and my son sometimes." A pain shadow crossed Thanopolous's face, made him pause in his work. "David's gone now, too. Desert Storm."

"I'm sorry to hear it."

"Wars like that, like the Iraq mess . . . stupid. Young men are the ones who pay the price."

"And their families."

"Yes. Well," Thanopolous said, and shook himself, and resumed his hammering. "You were asking me about Lloyd."

"He have any enemies that you know about?"

"Not Lloyd. No, sir. Everybody liked him. Especially the women."

"Ladies' man, was he?"

"Lord, yes. Had more than his fair share." Thanopolous chuckled—a dry sound, almost a cackle. "One thing he used to say. He was a dentist, you know, and he'd say, 'I fill cavities all day, and when I'm lucky I get to fill one at night.' My wife doesn't think that's funny, but it always made me laugh."

"Did he always have a roving eye?"

"You asking if he was a faithful husband? That's not for me to talk about. Nobody's business, now, anyway."

"Was he involved with any particular woman after his divorce?"

"Not that lasted more than a few months."

"So he never came close to marrying again?"

"Wanted nothing more to do with marriage. Divorce soured him on it."

"His lady friends. I'd appreciate a name or two."

"Can't oblige you. Sleeping dogs." The dry chuckle again. "Not that they were, any of 'em. Dogs. No, sir, he had good taste, Lloyd did."

Runyon asked, "Did he brag about his conquests?"

"Some, but he wouldn't give names or details. Gentleman about that."

"Brag to his sons, too?"

"No, never to the boys. Strict with them, as I told you. Kept his private life and his kids' lives separate."

"He ever bring a woman along on one of the hunting trips?"

"No, sir. Men only. Only time a woman ever showed up at the cabin, he chased her off quick."

"When did that happen?"

"Oh, a long time ago."

"Can you be more specific?"

"My memory's not so good anymore. Why?"

"I'd like to know who she was."

"Woman from Harmony, nearest place to the camp where you could buy supplies. Worked at the general store there, if I remember right."

"Can you recall her name?"

"No. Don't think I ever knew it."

"Why did she show up at the cabin?"

"Well, I'm not too sure about that," Thanopolous said. "Lloyd's the one who went out and talked to her. Said something later about her being a nosy female."

"Long conversation?"

"Not too long, no."

"She leave right away?"

"Pretty quick. Lloyd could be forceful when he had cause."

"How well do you think he knew the woman?"

"She worked at the general store, as I said." Chuckle. "You mean in the biblical sense? I doubt it."

"Why? Was she unattractive?"

"Just the opposite, as I remember. But much younger than Lloyd. He wasn't a man to chase younger women."

Runyon asked, "Did he go up to the camp alone very often?"

"Not often. Once in a while. Liked to get away by himself, same as we all do." Thanopolous finished tacking fine wire mesh across the frame he'd constructed. "Why so interested in Lloyd's private life and his hunting camp, young man?"

Runyon told him about the stolen photo album. "A lot of snapshots were taken on those trips, I understand."

"Oh, sure. Lloyd was a camera bug."

"Did he take any snapshots of the woman from the store?"

Thanopolous frowned. "Now why would he do that?"

"Just wondering."

"Well, I never saw one if he did."

"Showed them off, then, did he?"

"Sure. Just about every roll he developed. Camera bug. But there wasn't anything special about any of them. Why anybody'd want to steal an album full of pictures of fish and dead deer . . ." Thanopolous sighed, wagged his head. "Pretty frightening, when you think about it."

"What is?"

"All the crazies running around. Random violence. No wonder people are paranoid these days." He sighed again. "No paranoia in this case, though, is there? Some loony really is after the Henderson boys."

"So it would seem."

"You strike me as a smart fellow. Find out who and why, put a stop to it before something even more terrible happens. The police in this town never will. Incompetent, the lot of them."

Typical citizen's complaint. Thanopolous didn't expect a response and Runyon didn't offer one.

As he was about to leave, the old man opened a cabinet above the workbench, took down one of the jars it contained, and handed it to him with the air of a man bestowing a prize.

"Clover honey," he said, "best you ever tasted. No charge."

10

Jeremy Cullrane was a hard man to track down. When
I called the Pollexfen residence to confirm my lunch
date with Angelina Pollexfen, Brenda Koehler said that
Cullrane wasn't there and she didn't know where he could
be reached. He wasn't at the Bayview Club, or at least he
didn't answer the page I requested. He wasn't at Nicole
Coyne's apartment; an answering machine picked up
there. Another machine answered my call to his mail-drop
business number. I left messages everywhere, but by the
time I quit the agency to keep the lunch date I still hadn't
heard from him.

The restaurant one or the other of the Pollexfens had
chosen was called L'Aubergine, a celebrated French bistro
just off Union Square. Catered to the wealthy and to deal-
makers with unlimited expense accounts—high prices, designer food. Not the kind of place I'd have chosen, but
then I was not going to pay for the privilege of eating

there. If I had to pick up the check, it would go straight onto *my* expense account and Barney Rivera had damned well better authorize reimbursement.

Angelina Pollexfen was already there when I walked in at five minutes to twelve, in a cozy little rear booth with a martini in front of her. She wasn't alone. The man sitting with her wore a three-piece Armani suit and the kind of smooth, ultrawhite smile I distrust on sight. They made a nice pair. She was the blond, willowy type, gray eyes, creamy complexion, fashionably dressed; the diamond wedding ring on her left hand glittered and sparkled and had no doubt drawn envious looks from the other female diners. He was about her age, late thirties, his olive complexion darkened by heavy beard shadow, his black hair sprinkled with gray at the temples.

She gave me her hand, took it away again, and introduced her companion as "Paul DiSantis, our attorney."

"Do you feel you need an attorney present, Mrs. Pollexfen?"

"It's nothing like that," DiSantis said. His handshake was firm without trying to prove anything. "I'm not here in a legal capacity."

"Paul and I are old friends. We already had plans to have lunch today, so I asked him to join us." She favored him with a brief, crooked smile as she spoke, got another look at his dental work in return—touching each other with their eyes. Uh-huh, I thought. Friends. Right. All those daylong "shopping" trips.

He made room in the booth, keeping himself between me and Mrs. Pollexfen, and I squeezed in next to him. His leather-scented cologne was noticable up close, but it didn't stand a chance against the expensive French perfume that came drifting across the table from Angelina Pollexfen. I decided to breathe through my mouth. By the time the waiter came around, she'd finished her martini and was ready for another: "Double Bombay Sapphire, dirty, up, no olive." Two doubles before lunch—the lady was a boozer, all right. DiSantis seemed content with his glass of Pellegrino. I settled for black coffee.

Nobody said much by tacit consent until the drinks were served and we'd made our lunch choices. Mrs. Pollexfen knocked back a third of martini number two, licked the residue off her pink mouth, and said to me, point blank, "Well, did my husband accuse me of stealing his precious books? Is that why we're here?"

"No, he didn't."

"Really? Then he must have accused my brother Jeremy."

"Not exactly accused. Strongly implied."

She said, "Greg is full of shit," and knocked off another third of the gin and olive juice.

DiSantis laid a hand over one of hers, not being too familiar about it, and said, "Angelina," in a tone of mild rebuke.

"Well, he is, and you know it. Brimful to the top of his head."

I revised my estimate of how many doubles she'd had. What was left of the one in front of her was at least her third. No speech slur, but her eyes had a bright little glaze on them. Under the glaze, when she spoke her husband's name, something much darker shone hard and feral.

"If you feel that way about him," I said, "why stay married?"

"Why do you think?" She waggled the diamond for emphasis.

DiSantis said her name again, not quite so mildly.

"I'm just being honest," she said. "Greg doesn't love me and I don't love him. All that's holding us together is his money. What I can get of it, that is."

I asked, "Prenuptial agreement, Mrs. Pollexfen?"

DiSantis told her she didn't have to answer that.

"Why shouldn't I answer it? Yes, there's a prenup. And yes, that's why I'm still sharing my husband's house, if not his bed. If I divorce him, I get a small settlement and nothing else."

"You know you're no longer the beneficiary of his insurance policy?"

"Oh, he made a point of telling me when he changed it. He's written me out of his will, too, except for what I'm entitled to by law if I stay married to him."

"That could be construed as a motive for a half-million-dollar theft."

"Construe all you like. I didn't steal his damn books. Not that I wouldn't like to steal the whole lot and move to Brazil on the proceeds. That's all he cares about, his stupid collection." She drained her glass. "He's impotent, you know."

"Angelina." Sharp warning from DiSantis this time.

She ignored it. "For years now. Not even Viagra does him any good. He couldn't get it up with a splint for a pair of naked Hollywood starlets."

"Keep your voice down, for God's sake."

"Don't tell me what to do, Paul. You know I don't like it."

DiSantis was angry now. I watched him make an effort to hold on to his lawyerly cool. Pretty soon he said to me, "It's the gin talking."

"It's the truth talking," she said. "And yes, I believe I will have another."

"I think we'd better order lunch."

"Don't worry, it'll be my last. I won't embarrass you by puking in the soup."

"It's yourself you're embarrassing."

She signaled to the waiter. The filet of sole and another dirty martini, please. DiSantis ordered one of the specials — in French, no less. The only thing on the menu that appealed to me was a shrimp salad. Excuse me, *salade de crevette.*

When the waiter went away, Mrs. Pollexfen said to me, "My husband says you seem to be a very competent detective. Tell me, how do you think the books were stolen?"

"No idea yet. How do *you* think it was done?"

"Oh, that's simple. Isn't it simple, Paul?"

DiSantis had no comment.

"Greg took them," she said, "and hid them someplace."

"Why would he do that? He doesn't need the insurance money, does he?"

"Of course not. Money had nothing to do with it. He's a nasty, manipulative son of a bitch, that's why."

One of the women diners at a nearby table directed a

glare our way. Angelina Pollexfen stuck her tongue out in response. "Where's that damn martini?" she said.

DiSantis had given up on her for the time being. He sat in a silent, tight-lipped sulk. His body language said he'd make her pay for her bitchy and boorish behavior. By withholding his favors, maybe.

Her martini came and she nibbled delicately at this one, to make it last. The glaze on her eyes now was as thick as frozen syrup. "What were we talking about?" she asked me.

"Why you believe your husband hid his own books and filed a false insurance claim."

"To torment Jeremy and me, that's why."

"With false accusations, you mean?"

"Any way he can. He likes to hurt people he despises."

"You don't mean physically?"

"Oh, he's never laid a hand on me. Control, that's his thing. Hurt people by jerking them around, for his own gratification."

How much of that was truth and how much an exaggeration fueled by gin and hate I couldn't tell. "Why does he despise you?"

"Because I don't give in to him. I fight him every way I can. Don't I, Paul?"

DiSantis said, "I'm not going to let you drag me into this."

"Don't mind Paul," she said to me. "He doesn't approve of liquid lunches."

"Why does your husband despise your brother?"

"Why? Jeremy's an asshole, for one thing."

"Why do you say that?"

"Because it's the truth."

"Pretty strong comment about your own brother."

"He's a pretty big asshole."

"Must be a reason you think so."

"Two good reasons. He's a loser and a taker."

"Money, you mean? Bad investments?"

"Well. How did you know about that? Oh, of course, you're a detective. Detectives find out all sorts of things, don't they?"

"All sorts. How much of your husband's money did Jeremy take and lose?"

"That's not relevant to your investigation," DiSantis said.

"It is if Cullrane is involved in the theft." To her I said, "Those bad investments of Jeremy's. *Was* it your husband's money he lost?"

"Paul said that's not relevant. I say it's none of your business."

"Let's assume it was your husband's money, just for the sake of argument. And that the loss was substantial. Why would he let your brother keep on living in his house? Because of you?"

She smiled at that. "Hardly."

"Then why? Some kind of leverage on Jeremy's part?"

"Leverage. Isn't that a pretty word."

"I can state it more plainly."

The smile widened—a sly, knowing smile. Secrets. But she wasn't going to give me any hints; she stuck her nose in the martini again.

Lunch arrived. The plates might've been empty for all the attention any of us paid to them.

I asked her, "Does your brother need money now?"

"Everybody needs money."

"A large sum. For debts or another investment."

"I don't know and I could care less. Why don't you ask him?" Then, "Jeremy really didn't steal those books, you know. Any more than I did. I told you who's responsible."

"Let's assume you're wrong. Why couldn't Jeremy be guilty?"

"Isn't it obvious? Greg has the only key to the library and he guards it like the Crown jewels. Nobody but him is allowed in there. Nobody but him knows which books are the most valuable. Nobody but him could have taken them. QED. You know what that means, don't you?"

I let that pass. "What about you, Mr. DiSantis? That your take on the situation?"

"It does seem obvious," he said.

"On the surface. Somebody could've figured a way to get in when nobody was around. It only takes a few seconds to make a wax impression of a key, for instance."

"That's true, I suppose."

"If I didn't, and Jeremy didn't," she said, "who else is left?"

"Your husband's secretary."

"Brenda? My God, Brenda's so loyal to Greg it's a wonder she doesn't prostrate herself at his feet. Or offer to blow him under his desk while he's dictating, not that she'd be able to, poor thing. Did I tell you he's impotent?"

"Christ, Angelina!"

She wrinkled her nose at him.

I said, "I'd say she was more interested in your brother than your husband."

"Jeremy? And Brenda? He doesn't have much taste in women, but what he does have is better than *that*."

Like DiSantis, I'd had enough of her. Maybe she was easier to deal with when she was sober, but I wouldn't have put money on it. I shifted a little so I had a better angle on the lawyer and tried pumping him a little.

"What's your opinion of Gregory Pollexfen, Mr. DiSantis?"

"He's a client. What I think of him is irrelevant."

"How long have you known him?"

"Nine years. Since I joined Wainright and Simmons."

"And you handle his legal affairs?"

"The firm does."

"But not you personally."

". . . For the past three years, yes."

"Any trouble with him?"

"What do you mean, trouble?"

"Just that. Personal problems, professional difficulties."

"No."

"Visit him in his home?"

DiSantis didn't like this line of questioning. He said, "Are you trying to make me out as a suspect now?"

Angelina Pollexfen laughed.

I said, "Not at all. Asking questions, trying to get at the truth. Doing my job."

"Well, I'm not going to answer anymore. And I advise Mrs. Pollexfen to follow the same course. Do I make myself clear, Angelina?"

"Oh, perfectly. Clear as crystal."

"All right. Now suppose we finish our lunch like civilized people."

She laughed again, guzzled the rest of her drink, and winked at me—a broad, exaggerated wink.

"Isn't this fun?" she said.

When I made my escape from L'Aubergine, stomach grumbling, faculties more or less intact and credit card unsullied—DiSantis had picked up the tab—I sat in the car to decompress and check my messages. Only there weren't any. No callback from Jeremy Cullrane on any of the four I'd left for him.

I checked in with Tamara, to tell her about the lunch from hell and ask if Cullrane had called the office by any chance. No, but she'd picked up some interesting information about him.

"That deal I told you about yesterday?" she said. "It was for a music show at the San Jose Auditorium that fell through, cost everybody involved a bundle. Word is Cullrane was the biggest backer and biggest loser. One hundred large."

"A hundred thousand dollars? Hell of a loss."

"That's not all. He was a player in two other promotional deals since that went sour and cost him plenty both times. Man's a three-time loser."

"Where's he been getting the money?"

"Well, like I said yesterday, ain't no high rollers lining up outside his door."

"Any chance Nicole Coyne could be bankrolling him?"

"No way. The girlfriend's a lounge and club singer. Makes enough to afford a North Beach apartment, but she's not well off. Neither is her family."

"The money has to come from Pollexfen, then."

"Why would a man like him keep throwing good money after bad? He's got a rep as a tight-fisted businessman."

"And throwing it to somebody he admits he doesn't like or trust. Has to be leverage—the strong kind."

"Like blackmail?"

"Like that. It would also explain why Pollexfen puts up with him under the same roof. Question is, what kind?"

"Might have a business connection," Tamara said. "Pollexfen's not only tight-fisted, he's ruthless. Word is he plays fast and loose to get what he wants."

"Shady stuff?"

"Could be. Rumors to that effect."

"You find out anything more about his wife?"

"Some. She's a player, too, only a different kind."

"Men?"

"Yup. Doesn't seem to be too discreet about it, either."

"Names?"

"Linked to three or four guys. Paul DiSantis is one."

"Playing pretty close to home," I said. "Pollexfen has to either know or suspect, and yet he stays married to her even with the prenup and even though they seem to hate each other. She says the main reason is the community property laws."

"Good reason."

"And that he's a control freak, enjoys manipulating her, keeping her on a leash. Both good reasons. But I get the feeling there's more to it."

"Same kind of leverage Cullrane has?"

"The two of them blackmailing him together? That's possible. But then why don't brother and sister get along? She doesn't seem to like Cullrane any more than she does her husband."

"Maybe just a sibling thing," Tamara said. "Like with sister Claudia and me. Besides, you don't have to like a person to work a scam with him."

"True enough."

"Everybody hates everybody else. How'd you like to go to a dinner party at that house?"

"I wouldn't," I said. "The first big deal that went sour for Cullrane was five years ago, right? If he is blackmailing Pollexfen, that figures to be about when it started. See if you can find out if Pollexfen was mixed up in anything big and possibly shady around that time."

"I'm on it. Anything else?"

"Just the phone number and address for Pollexfen's collector friend, Julian Iverson. Maybe he can tell me something we don't already know."

11

JAKE RUNYON

The town of Sonoma was Old California, established in the days of the Spanish land grants, built around a central square with one of the original missions on one corner and nearby, the remains of a fort where troops were garrisoned when Sonoma was the capital of the Bear Flag Republic. Nowadays the historical aspects played a distant second to tourism and the wine industry. Expensive shops, tasting rooms, designer restaurants. And up-valley, dozens of wineries that catered to organized tours, charged ten- and fifteen-dollar tasting fees, and sold promotional items by the bushel.

Runyon didn't much care for upscale tourist traps. Too many people, too much traffic, too much undisguised greed. And too little regard for the residents. Prosperity bred high rents, overblown home prices, and jacked-up costs for goods and services. He'd heard it said that Sonoma was a nice place to visit but unless you had plenty of money and didn't mind crowds of out-of-towners, you wouldn't want to live there.

The Sunset Acres assisted living facility was on the southeast end, close enough to downtown shopping but far enough off the main road into town so that tourists wouldn't be reminded of one of their own potential old-age options. It took up most of a city block—small units strung together in wings radiating out from a central building that housed staff offices, kitchen facilities, and a recreation-dining hall. The units all looked alike, wood and stucco with tiny porches, and the landscaping was the low-maintenance variety crisscrossed by flagstone paths. Nothing special, nothing distinctive. Just a place for old people who had nowhere else to go and no family members who were willing to shoulder the burden of caring for them; a place to live out the rest of their lives in relative comfort.

Visitors had to sign in at the main building. Runyon had called ahead to make sure Mona Crandall was available and would see him, so he was expected. The woman at the lobby desk drew an X through one of the squares on a grounds map, doing it with a smile and a flourish as if it were the location of buried treasure. "That's Mrs. Crandall's unit," she said. "Number forty-one West. She doesn't have many visitors, you know. She'll be delighted to see you."

Not exactly true at first. Mona Crandall wasn't smiling when she opened the door to Number 41 West, and at first she didn't seem particularly welcoming. But he won her over without making any effort other than to be polite.

Reserved until she'd had time to take his measure, and then almost eager for his company. But not because she cared very much why a private investigator from San Francisco was visiting her, even though he'd made it plain in his call that his business concerned her two sons. Like a lot of the elderly in circumstances such as hers, she was starved for human contact and some friendly attention.

She was in her midseventies, on the frail side. Needed a walker to get around. Blue-rinsed hair that had had a recent styling and alert brown eyes. She'd been watching a talk show on television; as soon as she let him in, she moved over and switched the thing off.

"I keep it on for noise," she said. "Mostly what they have on these days is garbage."

"Except for old movies."

That earned him her first smile. "Except for old movies," she agreed.

She asked him if he drank tea. He said he did. No trouble at all to make him a cup, she said, and he let her do it, sensing it would hurt her feelings if he declined. While she was in the kitchenette, he took in the surroundings. The unit wasn't much larger than a studio apartment—small sitting room, smaller bedroom, bathroom, kitchenette. Furniture crowded the sitting room, leftovers probably from the home she'd shared with her late second husband. Television wasn't her only interest or recreation; a bookshelf was filled with well-read paperbacks and there was a stack of library books on the table beside her chair. Her body may have been wasted, but her mind wasn't.

When the tea was ready he went out and got his cup to

save her making two trips with the walker. Another smile. And they were ready for business.

She didn't know what had been happening to her sons. They hadn't told her and the only newspaper she read was the *San Francisco Chronicle*. "A terrible thing like that and I have to hear it from a stranger," she said. Concern in the words, tempered by bitterness. "Cliff and Damon don't call or visit very often," she said. "Keep to themselves. I haven't seen my grandchildren in over a year. They're all right? The stalker hasn't done anything to them?"

"No. Only to your sons. And their father's grave."

"Why, for heaven's sake? What possible reason?"

"No idea yet. It doesn't seem to stem from anything they did, their business or personal relationships."

"Well, they were always good boys. Honest, hardworking. They seem to be good parents, too."

"But not such good sons."

She sighed. "They blame me for the divorce. Breaking up our family, leaving their father to raise them alone. They worshiped him, you know."

"Yes."

"I tried to explain to them, when they were grown up, tried to tell them the truth. But they wouldn't listen." The lines tightened around her mouth. "Lloyd told them over and over that it was my fault, all my fault. That I was the cheater, not him. He poisoned them against me with lies."

The way Andrea had poisoned Joshua. Love your mother, hate your father. Love your father, hate your mother. Toxic damage that becomes so deeply ingrained over the years, it can never be undone.

"Cliff called me a spiteful liar to my face," she said. "I suppose I should be grateful they visit me as often as they do."

Grateful, no. But she'd been left with that much, at least. Andrea's poison had been lethal; Joshua was dead to him, no possibility of resurrection.

He said, keeping his face blank, his voice neutral, because this wasn't about him or his pain, "It must be very difficult for you."

"At first it was. Not so much after I met Wally, my second husband. He was such a good, faithful man. But now that he's gone and I'm alone . . . Yes, it's difficult. But I won't beg, not even for my grandkids. I didn't beg Lloyd Henderson and I won't beg his sons."

"How do you mean, you didn't beg Lloyd?"

"To stop cheating on me. I asked him, I threatened him, but I wouldn't beg."

"That's the real reason you left him?"

"Yes. I stood it as long as I could, for the sake of the boys, until I couldn't stand it anymore."

"A lot of women?"

"Almost from the beginning. One after another after another. He couldn't leave them alone. I gave him as much of myself as any man could want, and it wasn't enough. He had to have more, he had to have different."

Lloyd Henderson, pillar of the community.

"When that woman from up north came to the house," Mona Crandall said, "that was the last straw. A person can take only so much humiliation. Only so much."

"What woman, Mrs. Crandall?"

"One of his bitches. No, that's not right, I shouldn't call them that. They weren't bad women, most of them. He could be so attentive, so charming. I let him seduce me before we were married, why shouldn't they let him seduce them?"

"When was it this woman showed up at your house?"

"Twenty years ago. She was the reason I left Lloyd."

"You said she was from up north? Where, exactly?"

"Mendocino County. Some town I'd never heard of."

"Near your husband's hunting camp?"

"I don't know. I never went there with him and the boys. Hunting, fishing . . . I never liked killing things. Lloyd did. He made the boys like it, too."

"What did she want, this woman?"

Mona Crandall didn't seem to hear the question. Her eyes were distant, fixed on the teacup, as if the past were visible to her in the dark liquid. "He never wanted me to go with him. Took his women there, I knew that. All those weekends . . . it wasn't always his men friends he went with, it was his women, too."

Runyon waited until she blinked and focused on him again, then repeated his question. "What did the woman want, Mrs. Crandall?"

"Lloyd. She wanted him. She said she was in love with him, pregnant by him. He'd made promises to her, she . . . oh, I don't remember everything she said. It was a shock, you know. Being confronted with his cheating like that, so suddenly and right in my face."

"What did you do?"

"What could I do? Sent her away, sent her to him at his

office. He was furious when he came home—furious with me, as if I was at fault. We had a terrible fight. That was the end for me. I left him the next day."

"Do you remember the woman's name?"

"No. It was such a long time ago."

"If she was pregnant, do you know if she had the child?"

"No. What does it matter now?"

"It may have a bearing on what's been happening to your sons."

"After more than twenty years?" The bitterness returned to her voice. "Lloyd has been dead . . . what is it, five or six years now? Cliff and Damon didn't tell me when he died, I had to find out from a friend here. I wouldn't have gone to his funeral anyway, but they should have told me. Don't you think they should have told me?"

"Yes. I do."

"Past sins catching up. Is that what you're saying?"

Runyon nodded. "Past sins," he said, and let it go at that.

He finished his tea, refused a second cup. The refusal put a brief sadness in her eyes; she'd hoped he would stay longer. But she didn't make an issue of it. She'd been left alone so often in her life, by loved ones and strangers alike, that she'd come to accept it and the pain that went with it as her lot.

He was at the door when she said abruptly, "Mr. Runyon."

"Yes?"

"I remember now. Her name, the woman who came looking for Lloyd. Jenny. I'm sure that's what it was."

"Last name?"

"I don't believe she gave it. Jenny, that was all."

Tamara was skeptical at first. "Lloyd Henderson's bastard son? I dunno, Jake. Why would he just show up all of a sudden, after twenty years, and start throwing acid at his half brothers?"

"Say he only recently learned Henderson was his father and went to Los Alegres to confront him—money, payback. Say he's mentally unstable. Finding out Henderson's been dead for five years throws him into a rage. He takes it out on the old man's grave, but that doesn't satisfy him. So he goes after the two legitimate sons."

"Stalking them with acid just because Pop's been underground for five years? Sounds far-fetched."

"Depends on the details. What happened with Henderson and his mother, what his life was like, how he found out the truth. Kids can build up a lot of hate for a parent they think abandoned them." He thought but didn't say: I ought to know.

"So what do you want to do? Go up to Mendocino?"

"Worth the trip," Runyon said. "It's the only lead I've got."

"When?"

"Right away. I can make the drive in a couple of hours. Spend the night, start checking first thing in the morning."

"All right, go for it. You tell the clients about any of this yet?"

"No. Not until I see if the lead goes anywhere. The

hunting camp is near a village called Harmony. Can you get me the exact location?"

"County tax records and MapQuest—no problem."

"I've got my laptop. E-mail the info and I'll pick it up when I get to a motel."

12

Julian Iverson lived in Pacific Heights not far from my old apartment, but three streets higher—a much more rarified atmosphere. My place had been four rooms in a venerable, rent-controlled building with a snippet of a view from one bay window; Iverson's condo was on the fourth floor of a newly renovated low-rise, had seven rooms and unobstructed views of the Golden Gate Bridge and Alcatraz, and had probably cost him a couple of million dollars.

Three of the interior rooms were partially walled with books, less than half as many as Pollexfen had accumulated, but they weren't Iverson's only interest. He also had a taste for antique furniture, paintings, etchings, and other artwork, and Oriental carpets—rare Sarouks, a fact I wouldn't have known if he hadn't made a point of saying so. More proud of the carpets, it seemed, than his books. All he said about the collection, with a casual sweeping gesture as we entered, was, "Children's literature and fine bindings. My specialty."

He was seventy, but he could have passed for fifty-five or so. Lean, fit, his face smooth, his hair still thick and dark except for threads of gray. He'd been accommodating on the phone: "Greg told me to expect a call from you. Come by any time." He was just as accommodating in person, soft-spoken and cordial. We did our talking in a room dominated by fine bindings and half a dozen tasteful paintings of nudes in bucolic settings.

"How long have you known Gregory Pollexfen, Mr. Iverson?"

"Nearly thirty years. We met at an ABAA book fair."

"Close friends, then?"

"I wouldn't say that. We're both avid bibliophiles—that's the basis for our friendship. We have little else in common."

"So you don't socialize?"

"No. He comes here and I visit him at his home, to talk books. I'm a widower, you see."

A fact I already knew from Tamara's research. I nodded and said, "Your collecting interests are quite a bit different."

"True, but our passion for first editions is what drew us together and keeps the friendship alive. Greg may collect nothing but crime fiction, but his knowledge and interest exceed his specialty. As do mine."

"How would you characterize the man?"

Iverson smiled. "Passionate, as I said. Intense. Competitive. Generous when it suits him."

"His wife considers him manipulative."

"Does she? Well, she's probably right. I've known him to be devious and scheming when he lusted after a particular book."

"Would you say he's honest?"

"Are you asking if I think it's possible he filed a false theft report and a false insurance claim?"

"Indirectly, yes."

"Anything is possible," Iverson said.

"That's not an answer."

"No, I suppose it isn't. Let me put it this way. If Greg had a compelling reason for pretending some of his most valuable collectibles had been stolen in order to bilk half a million dollars from his insurance company, then the honest answer is yes, he might well be capable of it."

"But you don't think that's the case."

"No, I don't. He doesn't need the money, God knows. And I can't think of any other reason why he would fake the theft. He cares too much about his books to want to jeopardize prize items like the Hammetts and Doyle in any way."

"If they were stolen, then, who would you say is the most likely candidate?"

"I wouldn't. Other than it would have to be someone with access to both his house and library. And to the library key."

"Even though he keeps the key close to him day and night."

"I've been in that room several times. There's simply no way anyone could get in and out without one."

"His wife or his brother-in-law, then."

"That would seem to be the case."

"What can you tell me about Mrs. Pollexfen?"

"Very little, I'm afraid. We don't socialize, as I told you. I've only spoken to the woman a few times."

"Your impression of her?"

His smile, this time, was slightly bent. "I wouldn't care to say."

"What about Jeremy Cullrane?"

"The same. I barely know the man."

"Mr. Pollexfen considers him the prime suspect."

"Well, Greg is in a position to make that judgment."

"I understand Cullrane lost a large amount of money in a promotional scheme that backfired a few years ago. Music show at the San Jose Auditorium. Would you happen to know if Pollexfen was involved in that?"

"No, I wouldn't. We don't discuss business or personal matters, his or mine."

"Only books?"

"Only books."

"Assuming the eight volumes were stolen by someone other than Pollexfen, how likely is it that they'll turn up on the collectors' market?"

"Not very, I'm afraid," Iverson said. "Rare first editions in dust wrapper, in fine or near fine condition, are seldom offered for sale these days. Personal inscriptions are, of course, unique—especially those of an associational nature."

"By associational you mean books inscribed to fellow writers."

"Correct. Greg has notified all the reputable dealers and collectors in his field. If any of the missing items were to be brought to them, they would be instantly recognizable and the thief easily caught. Anyone with even a rudimentary knowledge of first editions would understand this."

"So he or she would attempt to sell them to an unscrupulous dealer or collector."

"Of which, I'm sorry to say, there are many."

"How easy would it be for a noncollector to find someone like that? Someone with enough money to afford to buy stolen first editions?"

"Moderately difficult, but by no means impossible," Iverson said. "Any sort of inquiry would have to be done sub rosa, of course, to avoid word leaking out. But a buyer could be found. And a price arranged before the books were actually taken."

All of which pretty much confirmed what Pollexfen had told me. Nothing new here, no insights or potential leads. Pollexfen, his wife, his brother-in-law . . . one of them had to be reponsible. But without either a clear-cut motive or answers to the questions of access and disposability, how to determine which one?

I got my crack at Jeremy Cullrane later that afternoon. After I left Iverson, I checked for callback messages and there weren't any. So I made follow-up calls to his contact numbers, and the one to Nicole Coyne's apartment paid off. She was there and so was Cullrane. She put him on the line and he said casually, "Oh, I got your messages. Just haven't had time to get back to you."

Meaning he didn't think it was important enough to bother. Meaning I wasn't going to like him any more than either of the Pollexfens did.

I prodded him until he agreed to let me come there "and get this damn nonsense over with." Nicole Coyne's apartment building was on Powell across from the North Beach playground; I found a place to park after twenty minutes of frustrated hunting, waited to be admitted to the building with an edge on my temper, and was greeted by boredom on the Coyne woman's part and sneering indifference on Cullrane's.

They were some pair, the low kind you'd rather discard than draw two. She was one of those slinky types, dark in a way that suggested Latin blood, sloe-eyed and exuding sexuality. Self-involved, though. She looked right through me, as she would any man who didn't have something to offer her, professionally, monetarily, or physically. He was tall and rangy and long-armed, blond like his sister, with the kind of elongated, knobby features that border on ugliness and some women find appealing. His charm was all superficial—the bullshit variety. So was the aura of superiority he projected. Unlikable, all right. More so every minute I spent with him.

The apartment was cluttered and reflective of Nicole Coyne's profession and personality: piano, recording equipment, show posters and blown-up photographs of live performances that featured her. A liberally stocked wet bar stood at one wall. The two of them had glasses in their hands when I came in, and judging from their eyes and faintly flushed cheeks, they'd been at it for a while.

No slurred words or motor impairment, though. Hard drinkers, like Angelina Pollexfen.

The Coyne woman sat at the piano, noodling with the keys, alternately sipping her drink and humming to herself, while Cullrane and I had our little talk. Nobody had asked me to sit down, but I wouldn't have anyway because he stayed on his feet the whole time, leaning indolently against the wet bar so he had easy access to the bottle of single-malt scotch on its top.

"Did Greg tell you I stole his damn books? Well, I didn't. As if I give a shit about a lot of old mystery novels."

"Valuable old mystery novels," I said. "Half a million dollars' worth."

"Oh, I'd love to have a half million. Who wouldn't? But I couldn't've gotten at them if I'd wanted to. He guards them like the gold in Fort Knox."

"Somebody got to them."

"Did they? Who?"

"How about your sister?"

He laughed. "Angelina isn't smart enough to plan a trip to the hairdresser's, much less a theft from a locked library. She's too busy cuckholding her husband."

"She doesn't speak highly of you, either," I said.

"She's a lush and a tramp and a liar, among other things."

"Not exactly warm and fuzzy siblings, are you."

"Brilliant deduction."

"Why the antipathy?"

"Chalk it up to differences of opinion."

"Before or after you moved in with her and Pollexfen?"

"That, my friend, is none of your business."

I watched him pour more scotch into his glass, nuzzle a little of it. "So what do you think happened to the missing books?"

"Obvious, isn't it? Greg spirited them away and hid them somewhere."

"Why would he do that?"

"Why do you think?"

"The half million insurance? According to his financial records, he's worth twenty times that much."

"Most of which is tied up in one way or another," Cullrane said. "Maybe he's got a deal cooking that requires cash."

"What kind of deal?"

"How should I know? The man's been known to take a flyer now and then."

"Like he did with you on the San Jose Auditorium show?"

A scowl turned Cullrane's knobby face even uglier. "What do you know about that?"

"The deal fell through and you lost a bundle. Pollexfen's money, wasn't it?"

"What if it was?"

"He doesn't like you and you don't like him. How'd you talk him into investing a hundred thousand in one of your promotions?"

"It wasn't all his goddamn money." Down went the rest of the scotch; the bottle clinked on glass as he replaced it. "I lost some of mine, too. And it wasn't my fault the deal went sour, no matter what anybody told you."

"You didn't answer my question."

"What question?"

"How you managed to talk him into making the investment."

"What makes you think I talked him into it?"

"He volunteered, then? Or was it his idea in the first place?"

"I didn't say that, either."

"You're not being very cooperative, Mr. Cullrane."

"Why the hell should I be?" he said. "My financial arrangements with Greg Pollexfen are my affair."

"They are unless they have a bearing on the case I'm investigating."

"Christ, man, I told you—Greg took the fucking books, nobody else. And you can bet he had a good reason. He never does anything without what he thinks is a damn good reason."

"Is that right?"

"That's right."

"But you don't have a clue what the reason might be."

"Also right. He's a schemer, you're a private eye. If you're smarter than he is, you'll figure it out like Mickey Spillane."

Nicole Coyne heard that and found it amusing. Not because she knew Mickey Spillane had been a writer, not a private eye, but because she was tight. Her laugh was low and throaty. "My glass is empty, Jeremy," she said.

He got up immediately with the scotch bottle. When he came back to the bar, he said to me, "You finished now? Nicole and I have an appointment for drinks at five o'clock."

He didn't seem to see the irony in that statement and I didn't enlighten him. "For the time being," I said.

"I've answered all the questions I'm going to," he said. "You come around again, you'll find me in my mime suit."

The Coyne woman thought that was hilarious. She was still laughing when I let myself out.

Frustrating damn case. No matter who I talked to or what information I came up with, I couldn't seem to move off square one. Some sort of crime had been or was being perpetrated here, but what kind? Theft? Insurance fraud? Filing a false police report for an unknown purpose?

Any of the three principals could be responsible. Pollexfen was reputedly devious, manipulative, and ruthless. Jeremy Cullrane and Angelina Pollexfen were money-grubbing alcoholics with secrets and manipulative behavior patterns of their own. None of the trio liked one another; accusations flew back and forth, none backed by solid evidence. Pollexfen had the means and opportunity to steal his own books, but no apparent motive. His wife and her brother had opportunity and motive, but no apparent means. Brenda Koehler? Opportunity, but no means and no apparent motive, given her spotless history and simple lifestyle. Julian Iverson? Neither means nor opportunity nor motive.

There was nothing to catch hold of, to follow through to a definite conclusion. One big confusing tangle of possibilities, half-truths, lies, secrets.

Where to go from here? The only option, unless Tamara uncovered something new, was for me to start over again: another visit to the Pollexfen house, to ask more questions, have another look around the library and maybe the rest of the place this time. If that didn't produce a lead, then another crack at the wife and her brother and Brenda Koehler—push them, play a little bad cop. And if that failed . . . quit beating my head against the wall, admit defeat, and file a report that would effectively approve Pollexfen's claim.

It would also prove Barney Rivera right and make him happy as hell, even if it cost Great Western Insurance the half-million-dollar bundle. The needle would come out, long and sharp, and he'd find ways to keep jabbing it into me for a long time afterward. The prospect was galling.

13

TAMARA

On the way home after work she detoured to Home Depot and bought some shelving, shelf paper, and a few other hardware items. The new crib on Connecticut on Potrero Hill had come furnished, but there were things that needed to be done to make it her own. She expected to be there awhile, and the small alterations she planned were the kind that would make any landlord smile.

The flat took up the second floor of a two-story Stick Victorian that'd been renovated and repainted four years ago. Two bedrooms, two bathrooms, kitchen, laundry room, high-ceilinged living room big enough to hold a dance party in. Good old San Francisco neighborhood, businesses and restaurants within walking distance—uphill from the flat so she could get plenty of exercise when she felt like it. Hefty rent, but not high enough to put a strain on the salary she drew from the agency. On the rental market just a few days when she looked at it. Pure luck no one else had snapped it up. She'd signed the lease on the spot.

The phone rang about two minutes after she let herself in. Probably Vonda. They hadn't talked since the weekend before last, when Vonda and Ben helped her move her stuff from the old apartment on 27th Avenue. Meant to call her last night, brag a little on Lucas and the solving of her little problem, but one thing and another had kept her from doing it. Young ho stuff, anyhow, bragging on getting laid. Vonda was married and five months' pregnant and all wrapped up in Ben and the baby. No more good-natured competition between them like there had been in their badass days. All grown up and respectable now. More or less.

Still, she'd probably have thrown out some details if it were Vonda on the phone. Only it wasn't. It was Lucas.

The sound of his voice put a smile on her mouth. When he left on Monday morning he'd said he would call, and she'd been hoping he would, that he wasn't just talking the usual man talk after bed games. But hey, this soon? All right!

"Thought I'd see how you're doing," he said.

"Doing fine. How about you?"

"The same. Any plans for tonight?"

"Put up some shelves, that's about all."

"I could come over and give you a hand."

Uh-huh. Give her a hand right into bed. The thought brought back memories of Sunday night and yesterday morning, and the prospect of a repeat performance or two made her tingle. "I wouldn't mind," she said.

"You eaten yet?"

"Not yet."

"How about I bring something with me? Pizza, Chinese takeout, whatever you'd like."

"Chinese sounds good."

"Any dish you're partial to?"

"Nope, I like it all. Surprise me."

"That's me at your door, in about an hour."

She put the phone down, still smiling, still tingling. Oh, Lordy, that man was good in bed. Better than Horace, she thought with a little satisfied malice. Better than anybody she could remember. He must've felt the same about her, wanting to come back for more this soon.

Sex was all it was, though. Each of them scratching itches. That was what she'd told Bill and that was the way it was. What she felt for Lucas was all below the neck. He said it was the same for him and she hoped he meant it. Last thing she needed in her life right now was another heavy relationship like she'd had with Horace. Love wasn't any big deal anyway. Overrated. Too many complications, too much chance of getting hurt again. Uh-uh. No, thank you.

She went out to the car for the rest of the shelving. Another nice thing about this new place: plenty of close-by street parking. The car sat there at the curb like a fat scabby bug: Horace's eleven-year-old Toyota. She hated that damn car—another of Horace's hand-me-downs, like the apartment on 27th Avenue. Get herself a new ride, that was the next change she'd make. And do it soon. Wash the last of Horace Fields right out of her life.

Back inside, she put the shelving and the other hardware items in the kitchen and then went around the flat straightening up. Lucas hadn't said anything, but she had a feeling he liked things tidy. Mama's influence, probably. She wondered again what Mama was like, how come a stud like Lucas lived with her and talked about her non-stop with that little glow in his eyes. Couldn't be anything kinky going on there, could it? Oh, come on, Tamara. Don't let the job make you suspicious of everybody. Man just loves his mother, that's all.

The flat was pretty clean, everything in the moving boxes put away the day after she took possession. Hadn't been much—clothing, computer equipment, books, CDs, personal items. When she'd packed it up she'd been surprised at how little she owned. Not much to show for twenty-six years of living. Well, so what? She'd never been all that materialistic. Money was nice, possessions were cool, but *living* was what mattered.

Making changes—that was important, too. Funny how one positive change could start a chain reaction. For her it'd been the decision to finally haul her booty out of that Horace-haunted apartment. Then she'd gone and gotten herself firearms qualified with Pop's help, as a safety precaution and so she could start doing some fieldwork again. Then, after weeks of hunting all around the city, she'd found just the right new place. And one week after that, she'd met Lucas and put an end to the long, frustrating months of unsatisfying sessions with battery-operated Mr. V. Next positive change: dump the Toyota for a new set of wheels, one that suited her and not that cello-playing chump in Philadelphia.

Happy again, life cool again? Yes! For the first time in

over a year, maybe for the first time period, because now *everything* was in sync, coming together at last. The new Tamara. Tamara Corbin, reinvented.

She put on a Dixie Chicks CD. "Not Ready to Make Nice"—God, she loved that song. Into the bedroom then, to put clean sheets on the bed. Nothing like clean sheets when you had somebody to snuggle down with. She dabbed some Chanel Allure under her ears and in the hollow of her throat. Not too much, just a sexy hint. Put on a nightie and a robe? Too obvious. Just let the evening play out like it had on Sunday.

She was sipping a glass of wine, listening to the Chicks, when the bell rang. Lucas came in with two sacks of Chinese takeout and a big smile. Kissed her, but easy, not aggressive. He wasn't in any hurry, either—something else she liked about him. Big and easy. Big all over, oh yeah! She always had been partial to big men. Ugly handsome. Blocky head, hook nose, hair starting to recede a little, but he had nice quiet eyes and a bushy mustache that felt like fur sliding over her skin. Thirty-four, he'd told her. Not too old. Mature. Exactly the kind of man she wanted and needed right now.

They ate in the kitchen, making small talk. Easy there, too—none of that awkward second-date stuff. She was curious about his work, what kind of sales job he had, but he didn't have much to say about it. Didn't ask much about her profession, either. Okay with her. Bill had taught her it was best to keep casual talk about the detective business to a minimum, except when you were dealing with professionals. So what they talked about, mostly, was Lucas's mama. Didn't bother Tamara, though it probably would if they'd been moving toward a long-term relationship. So the man loved his mother, so what? Kind of refreshing. Not too many thirty-four-year-old studs with slow, slow hands had a sentimental side.

"She's out on a date tonight," Lucas said, still going on about Mama. "I don't like the guy, but that's her business."

"How come you don't like him?"

"He's not good enough for her. Dresses cheap, talks cheap."

"Serious between them?"

"No, I don't think so. Casual."

"Like you and me."

"God, I hope not. I mean, you know, sex. I don't like thinking about her going to bed with that guy."

"Her business, like you said."

"Well, anyhow, it doesn't matter. He'll be gone before long and there'll be somebody else."

He said that last like it bothered him. Well, maybe it did, if Mama had herself a string of boyfriends. But she was entitled, wasn't she? Woman had been a widow a long time. A heart attack had snuffed Lucas's father twelve years ago, he'd said.

"I'd like to meet her sometime," she said.

"My mother? Why?"

"You talk about her a lot. She must be pretty special."

"Special. Yes, she's that."

Something in his voice again, but Tamara couldn't quite get a handle on what it was. Jealousy? Disapproval?

"Be all right with you?" she asked.

"What? Meeting Alisha? I don't know, I suppose so. We'll see."

Reluctant. She had the feeling he wouldn't allow it to happen.

A thought popped into her head. What if Alisha *wasn't* his mother, what if she was his wife? He'd told her he was single, never been married, and she'd accepted that without thinking too much about it. If Alisha was his wife, the reason he talked so much about her might be guilt working on him. Well? Come right out and ask him, he'd just deny it and spoil the mood. Did it really matter? On a casual hookup like theirs . . . no, it didn't.

Yeah, right. But good detectives were always looking for answers, something else Bill had taught her, and it was the detective in her that made her push it a little in spite of herself. "Okay if I ask you a personal question, Lucas?"

"If it's not too personal."

"Can't help wondering how come you still live at home. I mean, your mama doesn't sound like she needs somebody to look after her. . . ."

Whoops. Pissed him off. His face clouded up and he said, "Why I live where I live is nobody's business but mine and my mother's."

"Hey, I was just curious—"

"Well, don't be. We have a good little thing going here, Tamara. Don't screw it up by being nosy."

"Okay, sure. Sorry."

Took a few seconds for the anger to fade out of his eyes. Then he shrugged and the smile came back. "I'm sorry, too. I didn't mean to growl at you."

"No problem."

"Why don't we take another glass of wine into the living room?"

"Bedroom's closer," she said.

"On a full stomach? How about we just sit for a while, let the digestive juices do their thing." Slow wink. "Then we'll let the other juices do theirs."

"Cool."

The word reflected how she felt right now. Not as eager for those clean sheets as before. Another glass of wine, and if he didn't conjure up Mama again, she'd be ready—sure, she would. But there wouldn't be too many more nights like this one. She didn't care for that angry, private side of his. And Alisha kept cropping up and getting in the way.

Alisha.

Mother? Wife? Who was she and just what kind of relationship did Lucas have with her? Now she couldn't get the questions out of her head.

Well, there was an easy way to answer a couple of them, at least. Tomorrow at the agency.

Bad, girl, wanting to check up on a casual lover. Better not do it. Be smart. It's not important, it might put an even quicker end to the hookup. Don't ask, don't tell, don't really want to know.

Good arguments. She listened to them as Lucas poured wine, and nodded to herself, and made a promise to herself that she wouldn't do it—and knew she'd break the promise two minutes after she walked into the agency tomorrow morning.

14

JAKE RUNYON

Harmony was nothing more than a break in the two-lane county road. He came out of dense timber and there it was, like the appearance of a mirage—a scatter of buildings and a few hundred yards of surrounding meadowland. More thick forest walled it in on the east. Four miles in that direction, according to the directions Tamara had sent, an old logging road branched off and wound up to where the Hendersons' hunting camp was located.

You couldn't call Harmony a village or even a hamlet. The only public buildings were a tavern and a general store made of redwood siding and fronted by a couple of gas pumps. There was a house across the road, set far back at the edge of the meadow where cows and a sorrel horse grazed. Parts of a couple of other houses or cabins were visible at higher elevations among the timber.

The store and tavern were both closed. He should've figured nothing would be open this early, a little past nine by his watch. But he'd been too restless to hang around the motel in Fort Bragg, the nearest large town, where he'd spent the night. It'd been after dark when he pulled in there, too late to go out looking for Harmony and the hunting camp, and the downtime had weighed heavily on him. He'd left the motel at 7:00 a.m., wasted most of an hour on breakfast and a few more minutes driving around the area before finally heading out here.

He pulled over in front of the store, got out to look at the posted hours. Open at eleven. Two more hours to kill, unless he wanted to start knocking on doors hunting for the owner of the Harmony General Store. Better to use the time checking the Hendersons' property first thing instead of second.

He drove on through the close-grown stands of pine and Douglas fir, climbing gradually. The logging road was right where Tamara had indicated, 8.6 miles from Harmony. Rutted, and muddy in patches of deep shade, but not too bad; there hadn't been much rain or snow this winter. The Ford had all-wheel drive, so he had no trouble negotiating the rough spots.

Half a mile of bouncing and rattling brought him to the private road that led uphill through more timber and finally emerged in what appeared to be a man-made clearing. Tree stumps, old and crumbling from the assaults of insects and woodpeckers, spotted it here and there. He threaded his way among them to within fifty feet of the main cabin, one of three buildings that made up the camp.

He stepped out into biting cold and dead-calm stillness. Clouds and mist clung to the tops of the surrounding forest, as if somebody had draped them with puffs and streamers of gray bunting. Faintly, from behind the cabin, the sound of running water came to him—a trout stream that ran down to a small river whose name he'd already forgotten. He buttoned his coat against the chill as he moved toward the cabin.

It was the standard peeled-log variety, simple but sturdy-looking even though it and the two outbuildings hadn't been maintained over the past several years. High grass grew up along its sides, the A-frame roof was missing a couple of shingles, and one of the porch stanchions showed cracks and splinters. But it wasn't only simple neglect, he saw as he drew closer. The glass in the single facing window was broken, the front door stood a few inches ajar.

He went up and looked at it. A hasp for an old Yale padlock had been pried loose from the jamb, hung bent to one side. He pushed the door open. Two steps inside was as far as he went, as far as he needed to go.

The three-room interior had been torn apart. Furniture hacked to pieces by an ax or hatchet, the only escapees a flat-armed Adirondack chair and a small table. Canned goods split open and their contents splattered on walls and floor, glasses and bottles reduced to shards. But it wasn't just wanton destruction, the kind that kids or homeless squatters perpetrated. It was cold, vicious, calculated—a systematic act of hate or vengeance or both.

Burn holes and blackened streaks in the floorboards, wallboards. Pieces of glass and metal fused and bubbled. Acid. Flung helter-skelter after the first wave of damage was done.

The Hendersons' phantom stalker.

Runyon backed out, toed the door shut, and went to look at the outbuildings. One was a woodshed, about a third full; the cordwood had been kicked around and doused with the corrosive, as had the walls. Same frenzy in the second building. Padlock pried off the door, a couple of old sleeping bags and some blankets and other goods torn apart and burned with acid. And in one corner, the scorched remains of something that might once have been a wood rat.

The desecration of Lloyd Henderson's gravesite and the attacks in Los Alegres were bad enough, but this showed even greater levels of rage and hate. Any man capable of this kind of carnage wasn't going to be satisfied for long with venting on inanimate objects and rodents. Sooner or later, he'd start using his acid on human flesh.

Not quite eleven o'clock when Runyon rolled back into Harmony, but the general store was open early. Inside, he found the usual cramped hodgepodge of out-of-the-way mountain stores: hunting and fishing supplies and hardware items in one section, groceries in another. A burly, balding man was stocking shelves while a thin woman with hair dyed the color of French's mustard swept the floor. Both were in their sixties and wore the same style of plaid lumberman's shirt. The Fraziers, Ben and Georganne. Friendly and accommodating enough, but apologetic when Runyon asked them about a young woman named Jenny who'd worked there twenty years ago.

"Afraid we can't help you," Frazier said. "We've only owned this place four years. Bought it right after I retired from PG and E."

"Who'd you buy it from?"

"Man named Collins. But I don't think he owned it twenty years ago."

"He didn't," Mrs. Frazier said. "I remember he told us he reopened it about fifteen years ago. Closed for a while before that. Not everybody likes living in wilderness country like this. We love it, though."

"Does Collins still live in the area?"

"No. He was old, couldn't get around very well anymore. Moved down to Sacramento to live with his daughter right after the sale to us went through."

"Would you know who owned the store before it closed?"

"No. No idea."

"Any longtime residents in the area who would know?"

"Well . . . Mrs. Genotti, Ben?"

"She'd know," Frazier agreed, "but her memory's not too good. She's in her eighties."

"Anyone else?"

"Let me think. Twenty years ago, you said?"

"About that."

Before Frazier could respond, his wife said, "Oh, wait, Ben. That old desk in the storeroom—it's full of papers and receipts. There might be something in there."

"That's right. Might be at that."

"Would you mind if I had a look?"

"I guess it'd be all right," Frazier said. "Why'd you say you were looking for this Jenny?"

"Not her so much as a relative of hers."

"This relative do something wrong?"

"He may have. So you don't mind if I have a look through the desk?"

Frazier shrugged and glanced at his wife. "Georganne?"

"As long as you don't take anything."

"I won't," Runyon said. "Names and addresses are all I'm looking for."

They led him into the rear storeroom, then into an alcove that at one time had been used as an office. The scarred old desk took up most of the space and was piled high with cardboard cartons. More cartons were stacked alongside it.

"Have to move those boxes," Frazier said. "Okay for you to do that, but I'll ask you to put 'em back the way they were when you're done."

Runyon promised he would and began shifting the cartons around so he had access to the desk drawers. The Fraziers stood watching him, not offering to help. None of the desk drawers was locked. The usual desk clutter, some string-tied accordion files full of receipts for delivered goods and paid bills dating back to the midseventies. The only name on these was Harmon Digges, evidently the store's owner up until 1992. Runyon made a mental note of the name.

In the last of the large bottom drawers he found a stack

of dusty ledger books. One contained a meticulous record of charges and payments made by individuals who had been allowed to shop on credit. None of the first names was Jenny or Jennifer or anything similar. The second ledger listed payments made by Digges for various supplies, utilities, and services. In a separate section were pages headed Employees, Salary—and the name Runyon was looking for.

Jenny Noakes.

Employed from June 1984 to April 1988.

The salary record gave no address. He rummaged through the rest of the papers in the desk, hunting for an address book, social security and tax records—anything that would tell him where Jenny Noakes had lived during that period, her age, something of her background. Nothing. Nor was there any document that gave a clue as to why her employment had been terminated.

Frazier was still hanging around, watching him to make sure he kept his word about not taking anything and putting the alcove back in order. Runyon asked if the name Jenny Noakes was familiar to him. It wasn't. He replaced the cartons, offered to pay for the rummaging privilege. Frazier shook his head. "Not necessary," he said. "But if you're hungry, my wife makes the best deli sandwiches you ever tasted." Runyon wasn't hungry, but he bought a deli sandwich anyway.

Jenny Noakes. Up to Tamara now. All she needed to track anybody living or dead was a name.

•   •   •

His cell phone didn't work in the mountains; it wasn't until he was down near the coast that he was able to pick up the satellite signal so he could call Tamara. A few minutes later he was back in the old lumbering and fishing town of Fort Bragg. He hadn't had much breakfast; he found his way to a seafood restaurant under the long, new bridge that spanned the harbor entrance. He was sipping hot tea, waiting for a bowl of clam chowder, when Tamara called. He went outside to talk to her.

"Took a little longer than I thought," she said. "You'll see why."

"What've you got?"

"Jenny Noakes. Born Jennifer Torrance 1962 in Ukiah, married to Anthony Noakes June 1981, son Tucker born early 1982. Father listed on the birth certificate as Anthony Noakes. Looks like you were wrong about the kid's old man being Lloyd Henderson."

"Unless she was screwing around as a newlywed."

"Been known to happen. But she and the husband were living in Ukiah when the baby was born."

Ukiah was a long way inland across the mountains, the county seat at the eastern end of Mendocino county. Small chance she would have met Henderson there. He said, "When did she move to Harmony?"

"No record of her ever living in Harmony. But she and Anthony Noakes split up in eighty-five and she got custody of the kid. Aunt of hers lives in Deer Run. That's where she went after the breakup—same Deer Run address as her aunt's from late eighty-four to August eighty-eight."

Deer Run was about a dozen miles from Harmony. He'd passed through it going up and coming back.

"Where does she live now?"

"She doesn't. She's dead."

"When?"

"August of eighty-eight."

"What happened to her?"

"She was murdered," Tamara said. "Body found in the woods off a side road south of Deer Run three months after she died. Strangled and dumped."

Runyon digested that before he said, "Case solved?"

"Doesn't look like it."

"Suspects?"

"Can't tell you that. Online information's pretty sketchy."

"County sheriff's department the investigating agency?"

"Yep. I don't have a name for you, but whoever handled the investigation was probably mentioned in the Fort Bragg and Santa Rosa papers. Their online files don't go back as far as eighty-eight."

"What happened to the ex-husband?"

"Dropped off the radar in eighty-eight. Probably moved somewhere out of state. Could be significant, maybe—the date, I mean. Same year Jenny Noakes was killed."

"What about the son?"

"No record anywhere in the state of a Tucker Noakes. Unusual first name. Maybe it'll help track him down."

She had nothing more to give him, except for the address of the aunt, Pauline Devries, in Deer Run—177 Hill Road. He went back inside, looked at his cold tea and cooling bowl of clam chowder, left some money on the table, and took himself out to the car.

15

Gregory Pollexfen sounded pleased to hear from me when I called him Wednesday morning. "You have something to report, I hope?"

"Not yet, no."

"Well, it's early in your investigation. What did you think of Angelina?"

"Very attractive woman," I said carefully.

"On the outside. Did you track down Jeremy?"

"We had a talk."

"Arrogant bastard, isn't he? Guilty as sin."

"I don't have enough information yet to make that kind of judgment."

"Meaning you still think I could be guilty."

"I won't lie to you, Mr. Pollexfen. From my perspective you're as likely a candidate as anyone else in your household."

"I'm not offended," he said. "You're cautious and thorough—I admire that kind of detective work."

"I'd like to come by again, if you don't mind. Another chat, another look at your library."

"Would you? When?"

"At your convenience."

"Well, I have some work to do and there's a book auction at Pacific Rim Gallery I'm planning to attend this afternoon. Some rare Edwardian items I don't have in my collection. Would you be available late afternoon?"

"If it's not too late."

"Excellent. I'll check my schedule and call you back."

Tamara had been busy at her desk when I came in. Now she appeared in the doorway linking our offices. "Well, that's a relief," she said.

"What is?"

"He's not married."

"Who's not?"

"Lucas Zeller."

It took me a couple of seconds to identify the name. "The man you, ah . . ."

"Right. Never been married. Lives with his mother, just like he said."

"Checking up? He give you reason not to trust him?"

"Man's kind of closed off, you know? Doesn't like to talk about his job or himself, but he'll give you a ten-minute riff on his mama."

"And you thought maybe Mama was his wife, not his mother?"

"Occurred to me, so I decided to check. No big deal,

just curious. I mean, he's a lover, not a marriage candidate."

"Clean bill, eh?"

"Pretty clean, yeah. Works for Dale Electronics over in El Cerrito, been with them twelve years. He and Mama live in the Marina."

"So you're satisfied now?"

"Yep. Man's good for my bed as long as it lasts."

Modern young women. Outspoken about their sex lives. Don't worry too much about having an affair with a married man as long as he doesn't try to hide the fact from them. Don't see anything wrong in checking up on a lover, invading his privacy on the sly, to put their minds at ease.

There were times when the chaotic, permissive new world we live in seemed a little too much for a man of my old-school sensibilities. Inexplicable, too, in so many ways. Not to mention infuriating and depressing when the larger issues—insupportable wars, terrorism, rampant political chicanery, global warming, vicious anti-gay and anti-immigrant sentiments—came into play. It worried me sometimes, how out of touch and inadequate the modern world made me feel. Born a generation too late, past my prime, and too old and too set in my ways to make the necessary adaptations to connect with the ever-growing mess of changes and challenges.

Well, the hell with it. I'd made it a lifelong policy not to judge others' behavior or attitudes or lifestyles or political or religious beliefs, so why start now? And what did I have to complain about, anyway, when you got right down to it? I was still good at my now part-time job, a pretty fair husband and father, reasonably healthy and happy and content. There were a lot of people, whole nations of people, who were the real victims of the new millennium.

Pollexfen called back inside of fifteen minutes. "Would four this afternoon work for you?"

"Fine."

"Excellent. I'll send Brenda to the auction early and join her there after I finish with another matter. It shouldn't last past three, but if it does, I'll send Brenda to meet you and let you in. You won't mind waiting a bit if one of us isn't there right at four?"

"I'm used to it."

"Yes, I imagine a real-life detective would be. Mystery book sleuths all seem to have infinite patience."

"Mine's not infinite. Not even close."

He laughed. "Four or shortly after, then."

Strange bird, Pollexfen. I couldn't quite get a handle on him. His wife and brother-in-law were odd, too, but I had a better idea of who they were and what motivated them. Pollexfen was all shadows and smoke. His intimates kept calling him a manipulator and I had the same feeling about him. But what I couldn't figure out was exactly who and what he was manipulating, and for what purpose.

I pulled up in front of the Pollexfen home in Sea Cliff a few minutes early. I hate to be late for appointments, so as usual I overcompensated. At the curb ahead of me was a sleek silver Jaguar sedan; in the upslanted driveway, a new, dark red Porsche Boxster. I went up and rang the bell. No answer. Uh-huh. Back to the car, where I sat waiting and trying not to look at my watch.

Brenda Koehler arrived at eight minutes past four, driving a dark blue Buick. She parked behind me, and when we were both out and facing each other, she said, "Mr. Pollexfen is still at Pacific Rim." She looked and sounded a little harried, a little breathless, as if she'd run instead of driven from downtown. "There was one last lot he wanted to bid on. He should be here shortly."

"No problem."

"That's Jeremy's Porsche in the driveway," she said. "And Mrs. Pollexfen's Jaguar. Didn't you ring the bell?"

"Twice. Nobody answered."

"That's odd. If they're here, why wouldn't they answer?"

"Maybe they saw me and don't want to talk to me." Or, hell, maybe they were both drunk. Only four o'clock, but cocktail hour came early to that pair—very early.

The front door was locked. Brenda Koehler used her key, and we went into a cool, gloomy hush. In the front parlor, she asked me if I'd like something to drink.

I said, "No, thanks. But I wouldn't mind talking to either Mrs. Pollexfen or her brother, if you'd tell them I'm here."

"Certainly."

Away she went, and I moved over to stare out through the tall front windows. Gray outside—a wall of fog that obliterated ocean, bay, and all except the upper towers of the Golden Gate Bridge. The fog created a murky half-light that made the room seem even gloomier than the closed-in foyer.

Brenda Koehler was gone five minutes or more. When she came back she was wearing a puzzled frown. "I can't find them anywhere," she said.

"Neither one?"

"No. I wonder—"

There were sounds at the front door, footsteps and thumps on the tile floor, and Gregory Pollexfen hobbled in blowing on his free hand and looking ruddy-faced and much healthier than the last time I'd seen him. He said hello to me, pumped my hand, allowed as how it was cold outside, and then said to his secretary, "I see that Angelina and Jeremy are both here."

"Well, I don't know," she said. "I can't find them."

"What's that? Are you sure?"

"I looked everywhere."

His expression changed, darkened. "Everywhere? Did you check to see if the library door is locked?"

"No, I didn't think—"

"That's right, you didn't think."

I said, "I rang the bell when I first got here. If they'd gotten into the library, wouldn't it have alerted them?"

Pollexfen said, "No. The walls are thick—you can't always hear the bell with the door shut. Come on, we'd better have a look."

The three of us went into the central hallway, moving single file with Pollexfen in the lead, when the blast came from the rear of the house. Flat, percussive noise, like a muffled thunderclap, that jerked us to a halt for three or four beats.

Gunshot.

Large-caliber weapon, rifle or shotgun. I'd heard guns go off too often in my life, in too many different circumstances, not to recognize the distinction.

I cut around Pollexfen and broke into a run. He said something I didn't listen to, came clumping after me. I didn't bother looking into any of the rooms that opened off the hallway. The shot had come from inside the library. I knew that instinctively, without even having to think about it.

The library door was locked tight. I rattled the knob, beat on the panel with the heel of my hand. Silence from within. Pollexfen was beside me by then; he said, "My key," and when I turned toward him he shoved it into my hand. I jammed it into the upper lock, turned the bolt, yanked the key out, almost dropped the damn thing before I got it into the second lock and threw that bolt. It seemed to take minutes instead of seconds until I was able to shove the door open.

A wave of burned-powder stink rolled out at me. I plowed ahead, inside, sweeping the room, and then pulled up short with gorge rising into my throat. Behind me Pollexfen said, "Oh my God!" and Brenda Koehler let out a strangled little squeak, gagged, and spun and ran away somewhere with her heels clicking on the tiles.

Bad. As bad as it gets.

Angelina Pollexfen lay on the carpet in front of the desk—alive, her head rocking slowly from side to side, her eyes rolled up, little bubbling noises coming out of her. On the couch was a stack of books that had been pulled from the library shelves, seven or eight of them. Jeremy

Cullrane sprawled supine on the floor in front of the fire-place, what was left of his head resting on the hearth, the Parker twelve-gauge shotgun that had been hung above the mantel now lying half across his bent left leg. One barrel in the face at point-blank range. Blood and brain matter and bone fragments and blackened buckshot fouled the inside of the fireplace, the hearth, the carpet. The force of the blast had splattered more blood onto the books on the lower shelves to either side; it gleamed an evil crimson on the Mylar dust jacket protectors, clashing with the gaudy colors of the jacket spines.

I quit looking at Cullrane, swallowed against the rise of bile, and went to kneel by the woman's side. Conscious, but disoriented; her eyes still rolled up, the whites show-ing like pudding dribbled with flecks of blood. I'd have to get her out of here right away. No telling what she might do to contaminate the crime scene when she regained her senses.

Pollexfen said in a sick voice, "She killed him. Angelina . . . Jesus, she blew his head off. Why? Why?"

Yeah. Why?

16

The team of homicide inspectors who responded to Pollexfen's 911 call was reflective of both the changes in the SFPD's gender policies and the city's ethnic diversity. Senior officer: Linda Yin, a forty-plus, no-nonsense Asian woman. Her partner: Sam Davis, an African-American man ten years younger, heavyset and quiet, newly promoted from the way he deferred to Yin. Both seemed tired, a little stressed, a little short-tempered. Working an extended 8:00 a.m. to 4:00 p.m. tour, probably, and stuck with this late squeal that would mean even more overtime. I didn't know either of them and they didn't know me. But when I dropped Jack Logan's name, it bought me a certain measure of respect. Jack and I go way back to the days when we were both rookies fresh out of the police academy; he'd climbed the ladder the long, hard way to his present position of assistant chief.

While Yin and Davis and the forensics technicians

worked in the library, Pollexfen and I sat in the front parlor waiting for the inspectors to get around to us. Angelina Pollexfen was in a spare bedroom downstairs, where I'd carried her and locked her in—a precaution that hadn't been necessary; she was still only semiconscious when the law arrived. A matron and a police doctor were with her now. Brenda Koehler, sick and pale, had gone upstairs to lie down in another spare bedroom.

Pollexfen kept rubbing his hands together, a dry, brittle sound that scraped on my nerves. I wasn't feeling too well myself. Delayed reaction. A bloody homicide like the one I'd just walked in on always leaves me feeling queasy, tight-chested, depressed.

He said for the third or fourth time, "They were stealing more of my collection. Both of them working together. Did you see that pile of books on the couch?"

"I saw it." The one on top, I remembered now, was *The Talking Clock* by a writer whose name I knew from the pulps, Frank Gruber.

"Bold as you please," Pollexfen said. "You must have been right about a key made from a wax impression. There's no other way they could have gotten in."

If that was the case, the key would be on Cullrane's body or in Angelina Pollexfen's purse. No pockets in what she was wearing—something else I'd noted and had already mentioned to Pollexfen. I sat silently with my teeth clamped together, listening to the scrape, scrape of his hands.

"Why were they still in there?" he said. "They must have heard Brenda calling them."

Not necessarily. They evidently hadn't heard the door-bell.

"But why did she shoot him? An argument? You think that's it?"

"I'd rather not speculate."

"Deliberate? An accident?"

I didn't say anything.

"They must have been arguing," Pollexfen said. "One of them took the shotgun down—a threat. They struggled over it and it went off accidentally . . . you think that's the way it happened?"

"Your wife says she didn't do it, Mr. Pollexfen."

That came from Linda Yin, who had appeared in the doorway with Davis behind her. The two of them came into the parlor. "She's conscious now. Lucid enough to make some sense."

"Of course she'd say that. She's never admitted to a wrongdoing in her life."

"She says the last thing she remembers is having drinks with you and her brother over the noon hour."

Pollexfen blew noisily through his nose. "We had drinks, yes. The three of us. But she was fine when I left for the auction."

"What time was that?" Yin asked.

"Shortly after one."

"She and Mr. Cullrane both here then?"

"Yes."

"What do you think they were doing in your library?"

"Stealing more of my books. That's obvious."

"*More* of your books?"

"Eight of my most valuable first editions disappeared two weeks ago. I filed a police report, for all the good it did. They got away with those so it made them bold enough to go after more."

"How much value are we talking about?"

"Half a million dollars for the missing eight volumes."

Davis blinked at the figure; Yin showed no reaction. She said, "Insured?"

"In that amount. Eventually I had no choice but to put in a claim with my insurance company." Pollexfen gestured my way again. "That's why he's here. He's investigating the claim for Great Western Insurance."

Yin asked me, "Find out anything we should know?"

"Nothing conclusive," I said. "No sign of the missing books, nothing definite to point to the thief or thieves."

"My wife and her brother," Pollexfen said, "working in cahoots. That's obvious, too, now. I didn't think it was possible for either of them to get into the library—you've seen that all the windows are barred, and I have the only key to the door locks—but they found a way."

"Loose key in the victim's pocket," Davis said. He had a raspy smoker's voice. "It fits the locks."

"Made from a wax impression, probably." Pollexfen directed a grudging look my way. "Somehow one or the other of them must have gotten access to my key just long enough."

Yin said, "You say they were here when you left at one o'clock, nobody else in the house. Why do you suppose it took them three hours to go into the library?"

"I have no idea. You'll have to ask Angelina."

"What do you think happened in there?"

"The shooting? We were just talking about that. She shot him, on purpose or by accident—what else could it be? They were alone in a locked room."

"Premeditated?"

"I don't know, but I doubt it. Angelina can be cold-blooded, but not that cold-blooded. She wouldn't have the gumption. Most likely they had some sort of falling-out, one or the other pulled the shotgun off the wall, there was a struggle, and the weapon discharged."

"All of that with you and two other people in the house."

"The library walls are thick enough to act as partial soundproofing," Pollexfen said. "From inside you can't hear what's going on in other parts of the house unless you're listening closely and sometimes not even then."

Davis said, "It could've been suicide. Looks like the barrel was in his mouth or close to it when the gun went off."

"That could have been a result of the struggle."

"If he had his mouth open at the time."

"Suicide is out of the question, Inspector. You didn't know my brother-in-law. The man was incapable of self-destruction. He was the most self-involved, narcissistic person I've ever known."

"Sounds like the two of you didn't get along."

"We didn't. It's no secret."

"The shotgun belongs to you, is that right?" Yin asked.

"Inherited from my father."

"Kept it mounted on the wall above the fireplace?"

"Yes."

"Loaded?"

"Yes."

"Why keep a loaded weapon on display?"

"I really have no answer to that question," Pollexfen said. "My father always kept it loaded and I saw no reason not to do the same. The library is my domain. No one is allowed in there without my being present, and I've never permitted anyone to touch the Parker."

"Pretty large weapon for a woman to handle."

"Not for Angelina. She's fired it before, accurately. We used to go bird hunting together."

Yin seemed satisfied on that point. "Tell us again what you saw and heard."

"I didn't see anything," Pollexfen said. "Or hear any-thing except the shot when the three of us were in the hallway."

"And you could tell that the report came from the library?"

"It couldn't have come from anywhere else. We were on our way there when it happened. Angelina and Jeremy weren't anywhere else in the house—clearly they had to be in the library."

"The door was secured?"

"Double-locked, as always. The locks can be keyed from both sides."

"One key for the pair?"

"Yes."

"Who opened the locks? You?"

"I did," I said.

"My hands were shaking too badly," Pollexfen said.

She asked me, "You were the first into the room?"

"Yes."

"Mr. Pollexfen go in, too?"

"No farther than the doorway," he said.

"What about Brenda Koehler?"

"No," I said. "She ran off to be sick."

"Did you touch the victim or the weapon or anything else in there?"

"Only Mrs. Pollexfen. She was on the floor, moaning. Looked like she was suffering from shock."

"Blowing a man's head off would shock anybody," Pollexfen said.

"So you picked her up and carried her into the spare bedroom."

"While Mr. Pollexfen went to call nine-eleven, yes. Seemed like the best thing to do to make sure the crime scene wasn't compromised. Then I went back and locked the library doors again."

"Still have the key?"

I did and I gave it to her. She put it into an evidence bag, handed the bag to her partner, then the two of them went out into the hallway for a brief, whispered conference. Davis disappeared in the direction of the library. Yin stayed put, raised a beckoning hand toward me. "Come on outside for a minute."

I went out with her onto the front terrace. The street below was teeming with police vehicles and uniformed officers, the coroner's ambulance, a couple of TV remote crews, and the usual knot of neighbors and other gawkers. The thick fog and cold wind coming through the Gate didn't seem to be bothering them, but it chilled me in five seconds flat.

Yin gave the scene below a sour look and turned her back to it. "You have anything to add to what you told us earlier, what was said inside just now?"

"No. I've told you everything I know."

"You arrived a little before four, saw the Porsche in the driveway, figured somebody was home, and rang the bell. Right?"

"Right. No answer, so I waited in my car. Brenda Koehler showed up a few minutes past four and we went in together. She said the Jag down there belonged to Mrs. Pollexfen and the Porsche to Cullrane, so they were both home. I asked her to find the two of them—"

"Why?"

"Talk to them again. I interviewed both yesterday and I wasn't satisfied with the answers I got about the stolen books."

"Meaning you thought one or both might be guilty?"

"Not exactly. I wasn't satisfied with Pollexfen's answers, either. That's why I arranged to come here today—another talk with him."

"Why weren't you satisfied?"

"Well, only the three of them, and Brenda Koehler, had any kind of ready access to the library. One had to be responsible, but I couldn't get a handle on which. Or the motive behind the theft."

"Money. Half a million dollars."

"Not if Pollexfen took the books himself. He doesn't need to try pulling off an insurance fraud—not even for half a million. We did enough checking to be reasonably certain of that."

"Then why would he pretend to steal his own books?"

"Like I said, I don't have any idea. Just a feeling that he may not have been completely honest with me."

"Does he get along with his wife?"

"No. One big unhappy family."

"Reasons?"

"Lots of them. Complicated. You'd better ask Pollexfen."

"I will."

"Anyway, I guess I was wrong about him. Victim, not perpetrator, assuming his wife and brother-in-law are guilty."

"Assuming? Doubts about that, too?"

"Some," I admitted. "Unfounded, maybe."

"Let me be the judge of that."

"Well, Cullrane and Mrs. Pollexfen didn't like each other. Each of them made that plain. I can't quite picture them plotting a theft together."

"The dislike could have been an act."

"Could have, but I don't think so. Pollexfen confirmed that they didn't get along. So did the checking we did."

"A large sum of money can make partners out of enemies," Yin observed.

"Sure. I know it."

"You still don't sound convinced."

I shrugged. "There's one other possible explanation for what happened today."

"And that is?"

"Cullrane was alone, stealing more first editions, and

Mrs. Pollexfen came home and caught him in the act. But a couple of things argue against it. One, Pollexfen told me she never went near the library."

"She might have today," Yin said, "for the same reason you rang the bell. Saw her brother's car in the driveway and couldn't find him anywhere else in the house."

"True enough. But she couldn't've gone into the library unless the door was unlocked. And if it was, then why would Cullrane lock it—double lock it—after she was inside? I can't think of any good reason."

"Good point. Neither can I."

"Same question applies if the two of them were working together," I said. "Why double lock the door from the inside? Why not prop it open while they were gathering up another batch of books? That way, if Pollexfen or Brenda Koehler came home suddenly, they'd hear and have time to beat it out of there quick."

"Another good point. Any answers occur to you?"

"Not at the moment. Maybe Mrs. Pollexfen can sort it out for you."

"When she sobers up enough to tell a coherent story."

The house door opened and Davis came out. "Assistant coroner's done with his prelim," he said to Yin.

"Forensics?"

"Almost finished. Okay to release the body?"

"Go ahead." Davis went back inside and Yin turned to me again. "You can go now. All your contact numbers on the business card you gave my partner?"

"Agency, cell, and home."

"We'll need a signed statement. If you don't hear from us in the meantime, stop by the Hall tomorrow."

I said I would. She favored me with a tired professional smile and we went our separate ways, me to fend off cameras, microphones, and noisy media people on my way to my car. It took me a few more minutes to get out of there; a police car had blocked me in and one of the uniforms took his time about moving it.

Crime scenes: studies in organized chaos.

On the way home I tried to put the whole sorry business out of my head. None of my concern anymore. Chances were the cops would either find the eight missing first editions eventually or discover where they'd been sold. I'd send my report and expense sheet and bill for services to Great Western, and before Rivera authorized payment he'd jab me with his frigging needle and keep on jabbing afterward for his own amusement. My own damn fault for taking the case in the first place.

No, I didn't want anything to do with it anymore. But that didn't mean I had an easy time not thinking about it. Screwy business, full of all sorts of weird angles and nagging questions. The double-locked door. Why would Cullrane lock it if he was in there, alone or with his sister, to steal more books? And the time element. Why would they wait three hours to do the job when they could have done it immediately after Pollexfen left for his auction?

Didn't add up. Didn't feel right.

But you couldn't get around the rest of the facts. Irrefutable, or sure seemed to be. The two of them had been locked inside that room together—I knew that for an absolute certainty—and one of them was dead, and unless it was suicide, which was improbable as hell, the other one had had a hand in the killing. Had to be that way. Pollexfen and Brenda Koehler and I had been together when we heard the shot; that eliminated them as well as me. Unless some sort of gimmick had been used to trigger the shotgun . . . oh, hell no. You can't rig a heavy weapon like that to fire one barrel by using strings or wires or trick gadgets or remote control or any of that nonsense, and even if you could, Yin and Davis and the forensics people would have found it. The police aren't stupid. You can fool them, just like you can fool anybody else, but not on a crime scene like this one. Cullrane shot himself or Angelina Pollexfen shot him willfully or accidentally, it couldn't have happened any other way.

Still—it just didn't feel right.

17

JAKE RUNYON

Before he drove to Deer Run to talk to Jenny Noakes's aunt, he wanted more information on the homicide. He spent the better part of an hour in the Fort Bragg library, going through microfiche files of the *Advocate-News* and the North Bay region's largest newspaper, the Santa Rosa *Press Democrat,* for the latter half of 1989. Both carried news reports about the slaying, neither very long, and there was one brief followup in the *Press Democrat.* That was all.

The search produced one useful fact: the investigating officer for the Mendocino County Sheriff's Department had been Lieutenant Clyde Van Horn.

There was no listing for Van Horn in the local or county phone directories. So Runyon made his next stop the sheriff's substation, a short distance from the library. The young officer on the desk didn't know a Lieutenant Van Horn, but an older deputy on duty did. Van Horn was no longer with the department. Retired five or six years ago. Bought a place somewhere down the coast—Little River, the deputy thought it was.

Little River was about fifteen miles south of Fort Bragg, just beyond the quaint tourist-trap village of Mendocino. Runyon drove down there, stopped in at a grocery store and then a cafe. The waitress in the cafe knew Van Horn; he and his wife came in for breakfast now and then. She was pretty sure they lived on Crescent Drive, a few miles south off the coast highway.

Crescent Drive: short road that bellied out along the bluffs overlooking the ocean and dead-ended after a tenth of a mile. Half a dozen houses and cottages were strung along the oceanside. The first one he tried was deserted. A woman at the second told him the Van Horns lived in the last house before the dead end.

It was a small cottage built at the edge of the bluff above a rocky whitewater cove. Fenced garden in front, a lawn spotted with animal sculptures along the north flank. The Land Rover parked in the driveway told Runyon someone was home. The someone turned out to be Clyde Van Horn.

Van Horn was seventy or so, big, healthy-looking, and willing to talk. They sat in a living room that had two walls made of glass to take advantage of the ocean and whitewater views.

"Sure, I remember the Jenny Noakes case," Van Horn said. "You always remember the ones that go cold on you."

"She was strangled, is that right?"

"That was the coroner's opinion. Damage to the hyoid bone was consistent with manual strangulation."

"Sexually assaulted?"

"Undetermined. Three months in a shallow grave in the mountains, animals digging up and carting off pieces—there wasn't a whole lot left for analysis. No DNA procedures back then, not in a county like this one."

"Where was the body discovered?"

"Heavily wooded area about a mile outside Deer Run. Close to the road. County road crew was doing repairs and one of the workers went into the woods to take a leak and spotted the grave."

"East or west of Deer Run?"

"East. Why?"

"Curiosity. Turn up any suspects?"

"Her ex-husband seemed like a good bet—her aunt said there was bad blood between them—but he was working in an oil field in Texas when she disappeared. A couple of other possibles, but no physical evidence to lay the crime on either one."

"You recall their names?"

Van Horn thought about it. "One was a transient, young guy fresh out of the army. Potter, Cotter, something like that. Seen in the vicinity of the general store in Harmony where Jenny Noakes worked and was last seen. But he didn't have a rap sheet and his military record was clean, so we had to let him go."

"The other one?"

"Man named Jackson, worked as a handyman in the area. He had a thing for Jenny Noakes, kept trying to date her. She wouldn't have anything to do with him. They had an argument in a local tavern a couple of days before she disappeared. My money was on him, but like I said, there wasn't any way we could prove a case against him."

"Was she in a relationship at the time?"

"More than one, off and on. She wasn't exactly chaste. Liked men, liked a good time."

"One of the men Lloyd Henderson, owned a hunting cabin in the mountains east of Harmony?"

Van Horn had a habit of cocking his head to one side when he was thinking; he did it again now. "Henderson . . . sure. Doctor or something from some place down in Sonoma County."

"Dentist. Los Alegres."

"Yeah, that's right. Lloyd Henderson. Didn't you say the case you're investigating involves two men named Henderson?"

"Lloyd's sons."

"What, then? You think there's a connection between him and what happened to Jenny Noakes?"

"Maybe not with her murder, but Henderson knew her pretty well." Runyon related what Mona Crandall had told him about Jenny Noakes's surprise visit and pregnancy claim. "It wasn't long afterward that she disappeared, if Mrs. Crandall's memory is accurate."

"Interesting," Van Horn said. "I don't remember Henderson saying anything about any of that when I talked to him."

"You questioned him? Did he admit knowing Jenny Noakes?"

"Had to admit it. They were seen together in Deer Run."

"To having an affair with her?"

"He wouldn't go that far. Just acquaintances, he said. But that's what any married man would say under the circumstances. 'Specially if he knocked her up."

"But you didn't consider him a suspect?"

"No cause to. Spotless record, well-respected in his community. Everybody we talked to, including Jenny's aunt, said their relationship was casual, no trouble, no friction between them. If we'd known about the affair and pregnancy, we'd have leaned on him some. But the coroner couldn't be certain if she was or wasn't, as badly torn up and decomposed as the remains were." Van Horn cocked his head again. "You must've talked to Henderson. What'd he have to say for himself?"

Runyon said, "He's been dead five years."

"Five *years*? Then what could he or Jenny Noakes's murder have to do with his sons being stalked now?"

"No clear idea yet. But the first thing the perp did was dig up Henderson's ashes and pour acid on them."

"Man. So the real target was Henderson and his sons are, what, substitutes? Because of Jenny Noakes? That seems like a stretch after twenty years. Why would anybody wait that long to go on a rampage against the family?"

Runyon tilted a hand sideways. "I may be way off base here," he admitted, "but it's the only angle I have to work on."

"Well, suppose you're right and there is some sort of connection. Who could he be, this phantom stalker?"

"The perp's in his twenties—that's been established. Jenny Noakes had a son, Tucker, seven years old when she died. He'd be twenty-seven now."

"Sure, I remember the kid," Van Horn said. "Took his mother's death pretty hard. But I still think you're reaching. If it's the son all screwed up with hate and wanting revenge, why pick Henderson as the guilty party instead of one of the others I told you about? And why wait so long?"

"Recently uncovered some kind of proof, maybe."

"Such as what? Where? How?"

Runyon tilted his hand again. "What happened to Tucker after his mother's death?"

"Jenny's aunt took him in."

"The aunt in Deer Run? Pauline Devries?"

"That's right. Jenny and the boy'd been living with her since her divorce."

"She raised him?"

"As far as I know. I lost touch with her after a couple of years. That happens with cold cases . . . well, I don't have to tell you."

"So you don't know if he's still in the area."

"No, no idea what happened to him. You'll have to ask the aunt, if she's still living in Deer Run."

"I will. Did Jenny Noakes have any other relatives?"

"No male relatives," Van Horn said. "Another aunt, I think."

"Local?"

"No. I think she lived here in California, but I don't remember where. Or what her name was."

"Shouldn't be too difficult to track down."

"Internet, huh? Things sure have changed since my day."

Runyon said, "The changes come faster every year," and got to his feet.

"Listen," Van Horn said at the front door, "you find out anything definite about Jenny Noakes's murder, I'd really appreciate it if you'd let me know. That case has bothered me for twenty years. One of the few I wasn't able to close."

"I'll do that," Runyon promised, and meant it. There were a couple of cases he'd handled in Seattle he felt that way about. Still cold, as far as he knew, and a source of frustration in the empty hours when he couldn't sleep.

Deer Run, according to the sign on the western outskirts, had a population of 603. The village was strung out along both sides of the highway for a sixth of a mile — old buildings that housed a cafe, a couple of taverns, a few other businesses, and a newish strip mall at the far end. Hill Road intersected the highway just beyond the strip mall. It led Runyon up a sharp incline, made a dogleg to the left. The first house beyond the dogleg was number 177.

Only problem was, it had a deserted aspect and there was a FOR SALE sign alongside the driveway.

Runyon pulled into the drive. A chill, damp wind thrust against his back as he climbed the front steps, rang the bell. No response. He stepped over to look through an uncurtained window. The room beyond was empty of furniture.

When he came back down the porch steps, he noticed a woman in the front yard of the property across the road.

She was leaning on the handle of a weed whacker, watching him. He left the Ford where it was, crossed the road to the edge of her driveway, and called out, "Okay if I talk to you for a minute?"

"Not if you're selling something."

"I'm not."

"Rain coming. I need to get this grass down."

"I won't take up much of your time. I'm looking for Pauline Devries."

The woman straightened and gestured for him to come ahead. She was in her sixties, wearing a plaid coat, woolen cap, and work gloves. The wide swath she'd cut in the high grass along the driveway had a rounded sweep, so that she seemed to be standing in a miniature crop circle. Runyon stopped at the edge, smiling a little to let her know he was harmless.

"You a relative of Pauline's?" she asked.

"No. A business matter."

"Thought you said you're not a salesman?"

"I'm not."

"What kind of business?"

He showed her his license. She blinked, frowning. The frown used all of her facial muscles, so that her features seemed to fold in on themselves like a dried and puckered gourd.

"Oh, Lord," she said. "Not Jenny again after all these years? Jenny Noakes?"

"Her murder may be connected to a case my agency is investigating."

"So that's why you wanted to talk to Pauline?" The woman sighed heavily. "Well, I guess you don't know then. She passed away four weeks ago. Complications from diabetes."

Four weeks. That was why the address and phone listings still showed current. Tamara had accepted them at face value on her first quick check, and he'd made the same natural assumption.

He said, "I'm sorry to hear that."

"So was I. Friend and neighbor for thirty years."

"Then you know the boy she raised. Her niece's child, Tucker Noakes."

"Tucker Devries, you mean." The woman made a sour-lemon mouth around the name.

"She adopted him?"

"Year after the murder. Big mistake, you ask me. But she never married, never had any kids of her own. Maternal instincts got the best of her."

"Why do you say it was a mistake?"

"He gave her a lot of grief, that's why. Strange boy, moody, wouldn't talk to anybody for days, weeks at a time, not even Pauline." She tapped her temple with a blunt forefinger. "Not quite right in the head, and worse once he got into his teen years. All he ever cared about was taking pictures."

"Pictures?"

"Went roaming and sneaking around with a camera she gave him for his birthday, taking pictures of everything and everybody in sight. Told Pauline he was going to be a famous photographer someday. Hah! She was sorry when he left, but I sure wasn't. Nobody else around here was, either."

"When was that?"

"Must've been ten years now. Never even finished high school."

"He keep in touch with her? Come back to visit her?"

"Now and then he'd show up, when he wanted money. Not to pay his last respects, though."

"Do you know where I can find him?"

"No idea. Anna might be able to tell you—Anna Kovacs, Pauline's sister. She was in Fort Bragg for the services and out here afterward cleaning out the house. I asked her where Tucker was but she didn't want to talk about him. Acted like she wouldn't lose any sleep if she never saw him again."

"Where does Mrs. Kovacs live?"

"Some town near Sacramento. I forget the name." A sudden thought recreated the dried-gourd look. "Could be he didn't come to the funeral because he's back in some institution. Wouldn't be surprised."

"Institution?"

"Loony bin. They put him in one once, I don't know what for."

"Who did?"

"Police, doctors, courts—whoever."

"When was that? While he was living here?"

"No. Couple of years after he left."

"Where was this, do you know?"

"Nowhere around here, I can tell you that much."

"Did Pauline tell you why he was institutionalized?"

"She never wanted to talk about it. Well, she did say something once . . . what was it? Something about an episode."

"Psychotic episode?"

"Episode, that's all I remember."

After five by the time he got back to Fort Bragg. Misty, the wind herding in banks of low, scudding clouds that backed up the Deer Run woman's forecast of rain. The smart thing to do was to take another motel room here for the night, head out early in the morning. But that would make for another long period of down-time.

He hunted up an Internet cafe. No need to burden Tamara with the basic searches that needed to be done now. The agency subscribed to a bunch of different search engines, some more sophisticated than others, and he had the passwords to most of them.

An address for Anna Kovacs in the Sacramento suburb of Rancho Cordova was easy enough to find. Tucker Devries was a different story. One of those individuals whose lives are scattered enough to keep them off the radar. No easily obtainable address or employment record, didn't own property anywhere in the state, and his "episode," whatever it was, hadn't been of sufficient newsworthiness to make any of the papers with online files. Access to criminal records and DMV files was prohibited by law to private citizens, even those who worked for detective agencies, but Tamara had ways and means of getting the information. He e-mailed a request to her to pull up what she could on Devries.

In the car he started to call the number he'd gotten for Anna Kovacs, to set up an appointment for tomorrow. Changed his mind mid-dial. Better to interview her cold. People were more likely to answer questions about relatives face-to-face than to a stranger's voice on the phone.

The one call he did make was to Cliff Henderson's number in Los Alegres—checking in to make sure everything was all right there. Tracy Henderson answered, reported status quo. She wanted a progress report and he put her off because he didn't know enough yet to be sure he was on the right track with Tucker Devries. She and the rest of the Hendersons had enough to deal with as it was.

Choice to make now. Three hours plus to San Francisco, but then he'd have to fight commute traffic on Highway 80 to Rancho Cordova in the morning. At least a four-hour run straight through to the Sacramento area. As much as he liked to drive, it had been a long and busy day and with the weather turning bad, four hours was pushing his limits.

All right, then. Cut the distance to Rancho Cordova in half tonight, then stop at a motel somewhere. Two hours on the road was manageable, and by then he'd be hungry enough to eat and tired enough to sleep.

18

JAKE RUNYON

Anna Kovacs had no use for her adopted nephew, "that crazy little shit," and was reluctant to talk about him. Runyon had to do some fast talking, citing the seriousness of the situation with the Henderson brothers, to keep her from shutting the door of her downscale tract house in his face. At that, she wouldn't let him inside; they had their brief conversation on the chipped concrete porch. And he had to work to keep it focused on Tucker Devries. Mostly what she was interested in was herself.

"I wouldn't be surprised if he's the one you're looking for," she said. Large woman in her late sixties, heavily lined face, little piglike eyes pouched in fat. Too much lipstick made her mouth look like a bleeding gash. "Crazy, like I said. Nothing but grief for that poor dumb sister of mine. I told Pauline not to adopt the kid after brother Tom's girl was killed, but no, she had to be a mother. Well, she learned to regret it."

"In what way?"

"Didn't leave her house to him, like I was afraid she would. Left it to me, and rightfully so—I'm her only blood relative left. But up in the boonies like that, it won't be easy to sell. Not a single offer so far." She sighed and looked off down a street lined and cluttered with junk cars, pickups, stake beds, boats on trailers—metal-and-glass weeds in a decaying neighborhood. "My husband and me, we can sure use that money. He's a semi-invalid since his stroke. Needs constant attention. A burden, some days. A real burden."

"Where can I find Tucker, Mrs. Kovacs?"

She wasn't listening. "Pauline didn't have much in the bank, and her furniture and the rest didn't sell for much. Well, she never had much to begin with, just that house Tom willed to her when he died. Thirty years now, Tom's been gone. Construction accident. He would've raised Tucker if he'd been alive. Didn't take any crap from anybody, Tom didn't—he'd've raised that boy right, ironed out his kinks good and proper."

"Kinks," Runyon said. "I understand Tucker has been institutionalized."

"What? Oh, the twitch bin. Sure, more than once. They should've kept him locked up the last time. Better for everybody if they had, Lord knows."

"Why was he locked up?"

Disgusted snort. "Always taking pictures of people and not all of 'em clean and wholesome, I'll tell you. They caught him in Sacramento taking sneak pictures of women naked in their bathrooms, not once but twice, and the second time he went nuts when the cops tried to arrest him. Bit one, broke another one's arm. Another time he threatened some man, said he'd kill him if he didn't stop following him. Only the man didn't know Tucker from Adam's right buttock."

Tucker Devries: paranoid schizophrenic.

"All they done was lock him up for a while," she said, "and then let him back out on the streets. But that don't mean he ain't dangerous. My husband and me, we won't have him in the house."

"Obsessive about cleanliness? Washes his hands often?"

"Oh, yeah, that's another of his nut things. Says he can't stand dirt."

Paranoid schizophrenic with OCD—a bad combination.

"Last time I saw him," Anna Kovacs said, "he washed his hands right over there with the hose. And he wasn't here five minutes."

"When was that?"

"Three weeks ago. Come to pick up the trunk."

"Trunk?"

"That's all Pauline left him, his mother's trunk, and I wish she hadn't done that much. I hauled it back here from Deer Run, thought maybe we could use it for storage, and then her lawyer told me she willed it to Tucker. What else could I do but let him have it? Not that I minded, once I had a good look at what was inside."

"Which was what?"

"Clothes, books, photographs—Jenny's crap. Pauline kept it all these years, up in her attic. Never told him she had it. He seemed real upset about that."

"How upset?"

"Started yelling after he got the trunk loaded in his van and washed his damn hands, called Pauline a *b-i-t-c-h*. After all she did for him. Well, if that's what she was, I told him, then you're a son of a *b-i-t-c-h*. He said F-you and that's the last I saw or ever want to see of the little shit."

"Where does he live?"

"Vacaville. Up to last Christmas, anyway. Pauline had his address, probably wanted her to send him money."

"You still have the address?"

"No. I threw it out."

"What kind of work does he do?"

"Clerk in a camera store."

"Name of the store?"

"How should I know? I could care less."

"You said he drives a van. Make, model?"

"I can't tell one from another. White van, old, beat-up."

"Lettering on the sides or rear?"

"Just a crappy white van. Listen," she said, "it's cold out here, no sun again today, and I'm tired of talking about Tucker. You want him, you go find him. And when you do, do the world a favor and stick him back in the nuthouse where he belongs."

Vacaville. A little less than halfway between Sacramento and San Francisco, and some fifty miles from Los Alegres. Location of two prisons in the nearby hills: California Medical Facility, the state's health care flagship, and California State Prison, Solano. The medical facility might be the reason Devries was living in Vacaville; if he'd been remanded for observation to the psychiatric unit there, he could've decided to stay in the area after his release. One town, one clerk's job, was the same as another to a paranoid schizophrenic whose passion was photography. Vacaville's population was around ninety thousand. There were bound to be more than a couple of camera stores in a city that size, but not too many to make a canvass difficult.

By the time Runyon reached Vacaville, Tamara had called with the DMV and other information he'd requested. He'd guessed right about the California Medical Facility: Tucker Devries had spent nearly seven months there three years ago. Devries had a valid California driver's license and the vehicle registered to him was a fifteen-year-old Dodge Caravan. Height: 6'0. Weight: 180. Description from his license photo: round face, cleft chin, light-colored eyes, dark blond hair parted in the middle and worn in short, in-curling wings low on his forehead. Last known address as far as the DMV was concerned: 2309 Crinella Street, Number 11, Vacaville.

As for camera shops and other stores that sold photographic equipment, just a handful. Runyon asked Tamara to hold, took the first Vacaville exit off Highway 80, and pulled over long enough to write down the names, addresses, and MapQuest directions she gave him.

He made 2309 Crinella his first stop. It was in the older part of town, a residential street not much different in look or feel from the one Anna Kovacs lived on. More rundown, if anything. Cracked stucco apartment building, the two-storied kind built around parking areas and dead or moribund landscaping. Runyon parked on the street, considered arming himself, decided it wasn't necessary, and went into the central foyer where the mailboxes were. The box marked with the numeral 11 had no nameplate. He moved through the grounds until he found the unit, on the second floor overlooking a section of communal Dumpsters.

Half a dozen raps on the door brought no response. He tried the knob—locked tight. The window beside the door was curtained, the folds crossing fully from top to bottom so that it was impossible to see inside.

He didn't like the idea of bracing Tucker Devries at work, in a public place, but hanging around here on an extended stakeout wasn't an option. For all he knew, Devries was in Los Alegres planning more mischief.

Two of the local camera shops were in the downtown area. Nobody in either had ever heard of Tucker Devries. The third on the list, Waymark Cameras, New and Used, occupied space in a strip mall back toward the freeway. That was the right one.

The only person in the small, cluttered store was a fat man in a bulky turtleneck sweater who said he was the owner, Jim Waymark. He was all smiles until Runyon dropped Devries's name. Then the smile turned upside down, thinned out into a wounded glower.

"Yeah, I know him. He used to work for me."

"Fired or quit?"

"Neither. Disappeared without any notice. I came in late one day, he was supposed to've opened up, but no, the place was still locked up tight. And not a word from him since."

"When was that?"

"About three weeks ago," Waymark said. "I was thinking about letting him go anyway. He knew cameras but he didn't know how to deal with people. Get irritated, snap at customers for no reason. But I didn't take him for a thief."

"He steal something from you?"

"I think so, but I can't be sure. I've been around to where he lives half a dozen times, but he's never there. Left town, for all I know."

"Money?"

"No, a digital camera. Kodak EasyShare. I don't know why Tucker would've taken it, unless it's because it has the look and feel of an old-fashioned single-lens reflex camera like his old Nikkormat; there are a lot more expensive digitals in the shop. But the Kodak's gone and if I was a hundred percent sure he stole it, I'd've called the cops on him. Maybe I will anyway."

"Don't bother," Runyon said. "He's in a lot more trouble than you can make for him."

The first mailbox in the bank at 2309 Crinella bore a label that read: *Apt. 1 — J. Morales, Mgr.* Runyon found Number 1 and rang the bell. Ten seconds later he was facing a young Latina with a squalling baby slung over one meaty shoulder. Child voices and spicy cooking odors dribbled out from the clutter behind her.

"Yes?"

"I'm looking for one of your tenants. Tucker Devries, apartment eleven."

"Oh, him," she said. Another one with scorn in her voice. "The photographer."

"Seen him lately, say in the past week?"

"No. His rent's overdue."

Runyon flashed his license, handed her a business card; she looked at both with no expression, held the card between thumb and forefinger as if it were something dead and not very interesting.

"It's important that I find Devries," he said. "Very important."

"What'd he do?"

"Hurt some people. Might be something in his unit that'll help me find him."

Blank look while she rocked and patted the baby. It went right on squalling.

"It's worth twenty dollars to me to have a look," he said.

"Uh-uh. My husband, he wouldn't like it."

"Thirty dollars."

The dark eyes showed interest for the first time. "*How* much?"

"Forty. Best offer."

"Well, you know, I can't leave my kids alone here."

"Forty dollars for a twenty-minute loan of your passkey."

"Yeah? How do I know you'll bring it back?"

"You saw my license and you have my card."

She wrestled with her greed for maybe thirty seconds,

just about as long as it took the baby to stop crying and let loose a loud belch. Then she said, "Just a minute," and retreated inside and shut the door. Two minutes and the door opened again. In place of the infant she held a key on a tarnished brass loop.

"Forty dollars," she said.

He gave her two twenties and she relinquished the key.

"You better bring it back," she said. "And you better not steal anything or I'll call the cops on you."

Runyon made his way to Number 11, let himself in. Faint musty odor; nobody there for several days. He found a light switch. Room about the size of one in a downscale motel. Clean, tidy. Cheap furniture, nondescript, the kind you find in those same downscale motel rooms. The only stamps of individuality were on the walls—hundreds of photographs in orderly rows from near the floor to as high as a six-foot-tall man could reach. Mostly five by seven, some eight by ten.

He spent a couple of minutes scanning them. People, places, animals; fences, graffitied walls, junk cars. No rhyme or reason to any of them, except for two short rows on the back wall near the kitchenette. These were all eight-by-tens and displayed in the best location for viewing. And all depicted women—young, middle-aged, old—in various states of nudity, taken through bathroom and bedroom windows. Tucker Devries, the photographic Peeping Tom.

Nothing else in the living room. In the kitchenette Runyon opened the refrigerator. Half-full quart of milk nearly a week past its sell-by date. Eggs, packaged cheese left open so the ends were curled up hard, cold cuts, part of a loaf of sliced bread that was stiff to the touch and smelled stale.

The bathroom was outfitted as a dark room, the equipment neatly arranged on the cheap vanity sink, a red safe light in place of the bulb over the sink. He examined the bottles. Developing solution, fixer, stop bath. And one that didn't have anything to do with processing pictures.

Hydrochloric acid.

Tucker Devries was the perp, all right.

The only other room was a small bedroom. More cheap furniture in there. The nightstand, the bureau drawers, held nothing of interest. The closet was too small for more than a few items of clothing on hangers, a suitcase, a couple of cardboard cartons. No sign of the inherited trunk. Devries had either stored it or gotten rid of it.

Runyon sifted through the contents of the two cartons. One held photographs, bundled together and fastened with rubber bands. Discards, probably, ones Devries didn't deem worthy of display. The other contained his mother's belongings, some or all of what he'd decided to keep.

Letters. Wedding portrait of an attractive blond woman and a bushy-haired man, both in their late teens — Anthony and Jenny Noakes. Divorce papers. Baby pictures, and snapshots of a boy from toddler to about age seven. Locks of dark blond hair and other small keepsakes. A woman's hat made out of some kind of soft animal fur. Odds and ends that meant nothing to Runyon.

He thumbed through the letters. From Aunt Pauline and a friend in Ukiah named Darlene, mostly. A couple from men, short and suggestive of sexual relationships;

none of the names was familiar. Nothing bearing Lloyd Henderson's name, but two notes in a man's hand and signed with the initial *L*. One: *Can't wait to see you again. I'll be at the camp alone next weekend. See you then. Love.* The other: *Meet me tonight usual place. I want you so much!* Both notes written on what looked like letterhead stationery with the heads cut off. No dates on either.

Nothing there to indicate motive. Had Devries found something else in the trunk, more notes, maybe, that he'd kept with him or destroyed?

The twenty minutes were almost up. Quick looks through drawers in the kitchenette and the end table in the living room, and among a neat stack of papers and photography magazines on the coffee table, produced zip. There wasn't anything in the apartment to indicate where Devries might be holing up.

Runyon locked up, walked down and returned the passkey to Mrs. Morales. "If you see Devries in the next day or two," he said, "give me a call at either of the numbers on my card. It's worth another twenty dollars to me."

"Sure, why not."

"And if he does show, don't say anything about my being here looking for him."

"You think I'm crazy?" She surprised him with a conspiratorial wink. "I ain't even gonna tell my husband about the forty dollars."

In the car he sat for a time with his hands on the steering wheel, trying to figure his next move.

Los Alegres. Sure, that much was clear. If Devries

wasn't here, hadn't been here in a week or more, then that was where he was. But the problem was still the same one they'd faced all along.

How to find him.

19

I stayed away from the agency on Thursday morning, with the intention of doing the same in the afternoon. After yesterday's horror show I figured I was entitled. Write out my witnesss statement and drop it off at the Hall of Justice later on. Putter a little, read a little, catch up on cataloging my pulp collection. Quiet, relaxing day.

Yeah, sure. I should've known better.

I forgot about that insidious invention, the telephone. Silly me. If my brain had been functioning properly, I would have turned off the cell, unplugged the house phone, and drowned the answering machine in the bathtub.

The damn things, cell and house phones both, kept up a steady clamor from nine o'clock on. Three calls from Tamara. Three calls from media people, starting with Joe DeFalco, my old muckraking *Chronicle* buddy. Barney Rivera. Gregory Pollexfen. Even a damn telemarketer.

215

After the first two calls—Tamara, with a progress report from Jake Runyon on the Henderson investigation, and DeFalco—I wised up and cannily began to monitor the barrage of incoming calls. So I didn't have to talk to two of the relentless media, or the telemarketer. Or Rivera, whose sadistic imp I could hear lurking inside his message: "Call me. We need to talk." I knew what he wanted; Tamara had already told me he'd phoned the agency asking for a status report on the missing books and reminding her that the claim investigation was still open. I'd deal with him at my convenience, not his.

The other calls I answered. Tamara's second had to do with another agency matter. I picked up when I heard Pollexfen's voice because he sounded upset and didn't say in the message he started to leave why he was bothering me at home. Curiosity is sometimes one of my strong points, sometimes one of the weak.

"The police haven't found my first editions," he said without any preamble. "They searched Jeremy's records and the Coyne woman's apartment and there's no sign of them or what was done with them."

"So I've heard. That's too bad."

"Too bad? Is that all you have to say?"

"They'll turn up eventually. Or some evidence of disposal will."

"The police don't care about rare books. They won't even let me into the library to clean up the mess. Blood spattered everywhere . . . more than a few volumes may be irreparably damaged."

Some cold bird, Pollexfen. His brother-in-law had died in that room, apparently by his wife's hand, and his primary concern was possible damage to his books.

"Why tell me, Mr. Pollexfen?"

"Why? Why do you think? You're the only investigator I have any faith in."

"It's not my case any longer. The police—"

"Hang the police. What happened to my first editions is still an unresolved insurance matter. I've already spoken to Mr. Rivera at Great Western and he agrees. The investigation, your investigation, is to continue as long as the eight books remain unaccounted for."

That little son of a bitch. He'd keep me on the hook as long as possible so he could laugh all the harder when I failed. Well, screw him and screw Gregory Pollexfen.

"If it continues," I said, "it'll be by somebody else. As far as I'm concerned, I'm no longer employed as an independent contractor by Great Western Insurance."

"But you can't quit," he said angrily. "You *have* to keep investigating—"

I said, "No, I don't," and hung up on him.

The satisfaction was premature. I wasn't done with the Pollexfen case, much as I wanted to be; Tamara's third call convinced me of that.

"I just heard from Paul DiSantis," she said. "Wants to see you ASAP. Urgent."

"What about?"

"Mrs. Pollexfen. He says she's innocent. Says her defense team wants to hire us to prove it."

"Defense team?"

"Him and the criminal lawyer he got for her. Arthur Sayers. Only the best for the rich folks, huh?"

"Yeah."

"I think we should do it, and not just for the money. High profile, you know what I'm saying? Good for business."

Arguable, but I let it pass.

"I told DiSantis I'd get back to him as soon as I talked to you. Wouldn't do any harm to listen to what he has to say, right?"

I tightened my grip around the receiver's hard plastic neck and strangled it a little, just for fun. "My office," I said. "One o'clock."

Angelina did not kill her brother," DiSantis said. "She couldn't have."

"No? Why not?"

"Because she was unconscious for three hours before the shooting."

"Passed out drunk? Pretty flimsy defense."

He leaned forward in the client's chair. He didn't look quite as suave and self-possessed today. Angry, earnest, more than a little worried. He wasn't just playing bed games with Angelina Pollexfen, I thought; he genuinely cared for her.

"She wasn't drunk," he said, "she was drugged."

"Drugged? She reeked of gin."

"Two martinis, that's all she had. You saw how much she drinks—two martinis wouldn't give her a mild buzz, much less cause her to pass out. Drinking the last one in the library is all she remembers until she woke up in police custody."

"That doesn't mean she was drugged."

"The tox screen we had done does. Clonazepam. It's still in her system."

"What's clonazepam?"

"It's prescribed for anxiety disorders, among other things. A large dose mixed with alcohol makes a person sick and disoriented. And it can result in short-term memory loss."

"You must have told the police about this. What did they say?"

"That it doesn't change anything. That she took it herself, willingly."

"Well?"

"She wouldn't and she didn't."

"But she had a prescription for it?"

"Yes. For Klonopin, a trade name for the stuff," he said. "Her doctor gave it to her a while back, when she was having mild panic attacks at night. There's a supply in her bathroom medicine cabinet. She swears she hasn't taken any in weeks, and that she'd never voluntarily take it with alcohol."

"No? Why not?"

"She did that once and it made her sick. Very sick. She had to have her stomach pumped. That's not an experience anyone would want to repeat."

The time the EMTs had been called to the house, I thought. Matter of public record and a point in her favor.

"What's her claim?" I asked. "That her brother spiked her martinis?"

"No. Her husband. He made the martinis, but he drank scotch himself."

"So she's saying Pollexfen drugged both her and Cullrane?"

"She's not sure about Cullrane. We asked the police to have a tox screen done on him, but they said it wouldn't make any difference if clonazepam is found in his system, she could've given it to him as well as to herself."

"Why would Pollexfen drug the two of them?"

"Isn't that obvious? To frame her for the murder."

"How could he do that, Mr. DiSantis? Cullrane was shot in a locked room, Mrs. Pollexfen was the only other occupant, and I was outside with Pollexfen and his secretary when the round was fired."

"I know that, I know it doesn't seem possible. But I believe that Angelina is telling the truth. She didn't kill her brother. And she had nothing to do with those books being stolen."

"She think her husband is responsible for that, too?"

"Yes."

"Why? Why would he dream up such an elaborate scenario to frame Cullrane for theft and her for Cullrane's murder? What does he stand to gain?"

"He hated Cullrane and he hates her."

"There'd have to be more than that. And there's still the fact that he couldn't have fired the shot that killed Cullrane."

DiSantis spread his hands. "That's why I'm here. If

anybody can find out the truth and prove Angelina's inno-
cence, it's you."

"I'm not a miracle worker."

"Mr. Rivera at Great Western Insurance thinks you are."

Rivera again. I said between my teeth, "I'll want to talk
to Mrs. Pollexfen before I make any commitments. Has
she been formally charged?"

"Yes."

"Still being held, then?"

"Until tomorrow morning. Arthur has a court date at
ten to try to arrange bail."

"Can you get me in to see her?"

"Should be able to, yes. Now?"

"Now," I said. "I need to drop off my statement at the
Hall of Justice anyway."

San Francisco operates eight city jails, which says something about the local crime rate. Two of them are located down the Peninsula in San Bruno, there's a prison
ward in San Francisco General Hospital, and a pair for the
booking and release of prisoners and for "program-oriented
rehabilitation" are in the newest jail complex on Seventh
Street near the Hall of Justice. The other three are in the
Hall itself, on the two top floors. One of those, on the sixth
floor, houses the women's section where Angelina Pollexfen
was being held.

Every time I enter the Hall of Justice these days, I can't
help remembering that the sprawling monolith has design
flaws and is a potential death trap in a high-magnitude
earthquake. I don't read the newspapers as a rule, but

Kerry does; there was an article a few years ago in the *Chronicle* about the building's "vulnerability to calamity" that she'd called to my attention. The original structure was built in 1958 and has been expanded twice since, but none of the city administrators has seen fit to authorize the necessary retrofitting to meet current earthquake codes. There's been plenty of talk about putting up a replacement building, yet in twenty years plans haven't gotten much beyond the talking stage. The ever-increasing cost of tearing down the old and putting up the new back-burners it every time.

The Hall withstood the Loma Prieta quake in 1989 with only minor damage, though the power failed and prevented officers from opening an electronic door to the secured area where weapons are stored. In a stronger shake centered in or close to the city, the walls would probably crack and even if the building managed not to topple, or the section of the freeway approach to the Bay Bridge in whose shadow it sits didn't collapse into it, it would likely trap people inside and be rendered unusable—a crisis within a crisis. All of which makes me feel just a little vulnerable in its confines, despite the fact that native San Franciscans learn early on not to be intimidated by the threat of earthquakes.

The jails in the Hall are gloomy, noisy places presided over by grim-visaged sheriff's deputies of both sexes. DiSantis got us an audience with Angelina Pollexfen with no trouble, after which we went through the usual security checks and paperwork before being admitted to the visitors' room. A matron brought Pollexfen out and she and I sat down on our respective sides of the glass wall and picked up the communicating handsets. DiSantis stood behind me and, to his credit, kept his own counsel.

Different woman, Mrs. Pollexfen, than the one I'd had the adversarial lunch with on Tuesday. Orange jumpsuit in place of the expensive clothes, hair uncombed, pale face free of makeup, eyes sick and dull. The smart-ass cool had been replaced by a kind of wheedling deference.

"Thank you for coming," she said. "Paul said you would, but after the other day . . . I'm sorry about the way I acted. I shouldn't have had all those martinis."

I waved that away. "Tell me what happened yesterday."

"I didn't kill Jeremy," she said fervently. "I swear to God I didn't."

"Just tell me what happened."

"I don't know what happened. The last thing I remember is having drinks with with Jeremy and that bastard I'm married to. I started to feel woozy, I think I said something about it, and then . . . nothing until I woke up with police all over the place."

"Where did you have the drinks?"

"The library. I thought that was a little strange because Greg doesn't usually let anybody in there with him, especially Jeremy and me."

"His idea, this little gathering?"

"Yes. He insisted we be there at twelve thirty—he said he wanted to talk to us."

"About?"

"Those damn missing books. But he didn't really have much to say, just the same old baseless accusations."

"Against your brother?"

"Yes. And that I must have known and was keeping quiet about it to protect Jeremy."

"Were you?"

"No. I swear I don't know what happened to those books. Neither did Jeremy. He called Greg a conniving old fool and told him he'd better watch out or he'd regret it."

"Regret it how?"

Her gaze shifted to DiSantis, but she must not have gotten anything from him in return; she said to my right ear, "He didn't say how."

I said, "Look, Mrs. Pollexfen, if you want my help you're going to have to confide in me and in your attorneys. Everything you know, nothing held back. Understood?"

"Yes." Low, almost a whisper.

"The three of you hated one another, and yet your husband kept right on letting you and your brother live under his roof. I understand his reasons in your case, but not in your brother's. Did Jeremy have something on him, some kind of hold?"

No response for a time. Her lips were cracked and dry; she bit a piece of skin from the lower, scraped it off her tongue with a fingernail. Then, "He knew some things about Greg, yes."

"What sort of things?"

"Business dealings. I told you Greg was a manipulator. Well, his manipulations got him into a bind once and he did something illegal to get out of it. I don't know what it was exactly, just that it involved a small aviation company."

"And your brother found out about it, is that it?"

"Yes."

"When did this happen—the illegal act?"

"Five or six years ago."

"So your brother blackmailed him—"

"It wasn't blackmail. Not exactly."

"Call it manipulation, then. Manipulating the manipulator. That's how Jeremy got him to invest one hundred thousand dollars in the San Jose music show."

She nodded. "And when Jeremy lost the money, Greg hated him all the more. That's why Greg killed him and made it look like I did it—to get both of us out of his life at the same time."

"This secret. Can you give me any details?"

"Jeremy wouldn't talk about it."

"He never mentioned the name of the aviation company?"

"No. Wait, yes, I heard him talking to Greg once. Green something Aeronautics. Jeremy knew one of the executives who worked there, that's how he found out what Greg did."

"Local company? Bay Area?"

"I think so."

Tamara ought to be able to find out. I said, "Let's get back to yesterday afternoon. Your husband made the drinks for the three of you?"

"Martinis for Jeremy and me, scotch for himself."

"You said you felt woozy before you passed out. Your brother have the same reaction?"

"I'm not sure. I think he said his martini tasted funny, but . . . I'm just not sure."

"Where were you, the last you remember?"

"Where? Oh. Sitting on the couch."

"Your brother?"

"Beside me."

"Your husband?"

"In his desk chair."

"This was about one o'clock?"

"About that. Greg kept looking at his watch, saying he had to leave soon for some book auction."

"The three of you were the only ones in the house?"

"Housekeeper's day off and Brenda had already gone to the auction."

"The shotgun? Still above the fireplace, or did your husband take it down for any reason?"

"No. It was where it always was."

"Did he go near it, touch it?"

"No."

Three hours. Pollexfen could have put enough of the Klonopin into their drinks to keep them unconscious for that long. Shut them inside the library, go off to Pacific Rim Gallery, come back in time to keep his appointment with me. But how could he have timed the shooting so perfectly, with the three of us right there when the shotgun went off? Some way linked to how he'd rigged the crime in the first place? Maybe, *if* he'd rigged the crime in the first place. But how in hell could you blow off the back of a man's head when you were on the other side of a double-bolted door?

Angelina Pollexfen intuited what I was thinking. "I don't know how he did it," she said. "All I know is that I didn't. My own brother . . . my God, we didn't get along but I would never have threatened him with a loaded shotgun like they're saying. I couldn't kill anybody, not for *any* reason."

I believed her. Her voice, her body language, the haunted desperation on her face and in her eyes . . . they all said she was telling the truth.

Pollexfen, then.

I think maybe I'd known all along it had to be Pollexfen.

20

DiSantis and I parted company in the elevator and I went on into General Works and the Homicide Division on the fourth floor. Linda Yin was away from her desk in the inspectors' bullpen, but Sam Davis sat working at his. I gave him my signed witness statement, then asked if he had a few minutes to spare.

"Not really," he said, but he gestured me into a vacant chair anyway. "What's on your mind?"

"Couple of things. Gregory Pollexfen's missing books turn up yet?"

"No. We figure they were sold off right away. By the vic or Mrs. Pollexfen or the two of them together."

"But you haven't found any record—large bank deposits, large amounts of cash, that kind of thing."

"Not so far."

"Well, if you can't get some kind of trace, Great Western Insurance is stuck with paying off Pollexfen's claim.

So their claims adjuster wants me to keep on with my investigation."

"We don't have any problem with that."

"How about with me doing a little sniffing on the homicide? As long as I don't get in your way?"

"Better check with my partner on that. Why the interest?"

"I just had a talk with Mrs. Pollexfen, at her and her attorney's request. I think she's telling a straight story."

One of Davis's bushy eyebrows tilted upward. "Nine out of ten claim they're innocent."

"She could be the tenth who isn't lying."

"All the evidence says otherwise."

"Evidence can sometimes be misleading. We both know that."

"Sometimes. Not this time. Not according to forensics, ballistics, and pathology. We—"

His phone rang. Davis picked up, listened, pulled a grimace. "It won't do you any good to keep calling, Mr. Pollexfen. I told you, my partner told you, you'll have access when—What's that?" He listened some more. "Look, just be patient, all right? Tomorrow, probably, that's the best answer I can give you."

When he hung up, I said, "Pollexfen seems anxious to get into his library."

"Second time he's called, demanding his keys so he can clean up in there. If he wasn't a relentless pain in the ass, he might've got them back today."

Keys, plural. Pollexfen's and the duplicate found on Cullrane's body. Standard police procedure to hold on to them, to ensure that the room remained sealed in case another examination of the crime scene was necessary.

I said, "Can I ask you some questions about the evidence?"

Long study before he said, "My partner and I asked around about you. You've got a good rep for cooperation with the department."

"I was on the job myself before I went out on my own."

"So we heard. Go ahead, ask your questions."

"Nitrate tests indicate Mrs. Pollexfen fired the shotgun?"

"No. They came up negative."

"But positive on Jeremy Cullrane?"

"That's right. It could've been suicide—that's what her lawyers'll claim—but we don't see it that way."

"How'd it happen, then? She was threatening him with the weapon, he grabbed it and yanked it out of her hands, and the barrel jabbed into his mouth as it went off?"

Davis nodded. "Hair triggers on that shotgun, the pull lightened down to less than four pounds' pressure. Wouldn't have taken much of a yank with her finger on the foretrigger to fire the round when he jerked it up into his face as he was falling backward."

"Fingerprints?"

"Hers on the grip, stock, and barrel. Three of 'em, nice and clear."

"None on the trigger?"

"Smudges."

"Cullrane's prints on the weapon?"

"None that were clear enough to identify."

"How about burn marks on his hands?"

"No," Davis said, "but that doesn't prove anything. He didn't have to've grabbed the hot barrel. Could've caught the grip close to the chamber area."

"What about this drug, clonazepam, she had in her system? Did it show up in Cullrane's, too?"

"Yes, but so what? She could've spiked his drink and hers both."

"Or Pollexfen could've done it. He made the drinks."

"She says he did. Says he arranged the whole thing to get rid of her brother and frame her. You buy into that?"

"I think it's possible."

"Hell, man, you were out in the hallway with Pollexfen and the secretary when Cullrane died. And you were the one who used the keys to get into the library. The old man couldn't have done it, now could he?"

"Doesn't seem like it. I don't suppose there was anything unusual on the weapon—scratches, marks, some kind of attachment that didn't belong?"

"Nothing," Davis said. "Good condition, clean, oiled. What're you thinking? Fix an antique shotgun to fire by some trick? Can't be done."

"No," I said, "I guess it can't."

At the agency I asked Tamara to find out what she could about the aviation company business five or six years ago, and about the drug clonazepam. It didn't take her long in either case.

The aviation company turned out to be a Bay Area outfit, Greenfield Aeronautics. Hostile takeover by a larger outfit,

Drexel Aviation. Head of Drexel's board of directors: Gregory Pollexfen. Hints of bribery and coercion, but nothing proven and no criminal charges or lawsuits filed. Cullrane must have had some documentary evidence against Pollexfen to make the blackmail work. Had Pollexfen found out where it was hidden? Another possibility: whatever the crime, the statute of limitations had run out and he couldn't be prosecuted for it any longer. And another: his hatred for Cullrane had grown powerful enough to outweigh any concern over the consequences of his illegal business actions. In any event, the information gave substance to Angelina Pollexfen's claim.

As for clonazepam—

"It's a benzodiazepine drug," Tamara said, reading from her computer screen. "Used to treat epilepsy, anxiety disorders, panic attacks and night terrors, chronic fatigue syndrome, a few other things. Stimulates the action of gamma-aminobutyric acid on the central nervous system."

"Sure it does," I said. "Everybody knows that."

"Says here clonazepam is a highly potent variety of benzodiazepine because of strong anxiolytic properties and euphoric side effects. Use of alcohol while taking it intensifies these side effects."

"Which are?"

"Impaired motor function, impaired coordination and balance, disorientation, something called anterograde amnesia."

"Short-term memory loss, probably."

"Add all that together and you got one mother of a

hangover. You'd have to be crazy to mix up clonazepam and martinis on purpose."

"Unless you weren't planning to drink them yourself. Unless you had a good reason for serving them to two other people."

I sat closed inside my office, brooding. Pollexfen, not his wife—my gut said it and my head said it. But how could he have arranged the murder? There had to be some angle none of us had thought of yet. It wouldn't be fancy or complicated, either. Simple. The kind of thing that's obvious once you put all the facts together and look at them in the right way.

Yeah. Simple, obvious.

Except that no matter how hard I tried, I couldn't come up with any plausible explanation.

21

JAKE RUNYON

Los Alegres, early afternoon.

Duty and obligation dictated he take what he'd found out straight to the local police, but he was reluctant to do that just yet. He'd dealt often enough with small-town cops, been on the job himself for enough years, to know what kind of reception he'd get. The lieutenant, St. John, would be skeptical, tell him he didn't have enough hard evidence against Tucker Devries to warrant a BOLO, much less an APB. Plus he'd have to withhold some of what he'd found out because it had been obtained through a technically illegal search. If he could locate Devries first, he'd have a stronger case. Maybe not strong enough for the law to act immediately, but enough to get them moving. And to give himself a couple of options, if he wanted to pursue them. Confront Devries, try to prod him into an admission of guilt. Or put him under surveillance, stop him before he did any more damage to the Henderson brothers.

There were half a dozen motels in Los Alegres and vicinity, another couple of dozen within a fifteen-mile radius. Runyon began the canvass as soon as he'd made a list from the Yellow Pages in the county directory. The odds were only fair that Devries had decided to hole up in a motel somewhere around here rather than drive back and forth to Vacaville. He could be sleeping in that van of his, or crashing with somebody who didn't know what he was up to. But there were no other leads to follow. A motel search was the only proactive idea Runyon could come up with.

The places in Los Alegres first, and those drew blanks. North, then, to a stretch of motels at or near freeway interchanges. He skipped the more expensive chain places. Given the kind of work Devries did and the apartment building he lived in, he wouldn't have much money to spend on lodging. Or much interest in where he stayed beyond its proximity to Los Alegres; his whole focus was on his private vendetta. If he'd rented a motel room anywhere, it would be the cheap variety.

Two hours, nine stops—nine more blanks. Number ten was outside a little town eight miles northeast of Los Alegres, a twelve-unit, no-frills place built in a half square around a lumpy macadam parking lot. Twin Palms Court. But there was only one palm on the property and it looked ripe for a chain saw. Owner with a sense of humor or a substandard IQ.

The office was a tiny room bisected by a counter and presided over by a thin wisp of a man with gray hair just as wispy; a goiterlike growth on one side of his neck gave his head a misshapen cast. His smile was as thin as the rest of him. The bored, indifferent type.

Runyon had used the same opening so often he repeated the words by rote: "I'm looking for a young man, late twenties, dark blond hair, drives a white Dodge Caravan. You have a guest in the past week or so who fits that description?"

"This fella a friend of yours?"

"No."

"What you want with him, then?"

"Do you know him?"

"You answer my question, I'll answer yours."

Runyon showed his ID, and when the deskman had had his look, "He's involved in a case I'm investigating."

"He do something, break the law or something?"

"That's right. And he's liable to break it again if I don't find him pretty soon."

The desk clerk chewed on that for a time. Shrugged and said, "What the hell, then. Yeah, he stayed here. This past week and one time before that. But he checked out this morning."

"How long was he here?"

"This time? Five days? Let me check." Quick shuffle through a batch of registration cards. "Five days, right. Left early."

"Early?"

"Asked for a weekly rate when he checked in and I gave it to him."

"Mind if I look at that card?"

Another hesitation, another shrug. "What the hell," the clerk said again and handed it over.

In a weak backhand scrawl: *T. Devries, Vacaville*. No effort to hide his identity. The license plate number matched the one Tamara had supplied and "Dodge van" had been written in the box marked *Make of Car*. No credit card information: Devries had paid with cash.

"Any trouble while he was here?" Runyon asked.

"Not when I was on duty. Hardly even saw him. Seemed like a nice enough kid, said he was in the area on business. But I guess you never know, huh?"

"What time did he check out?"

"Little before noon. Twelve's checkout time."

Noon. Missed him by four hours. "Did he say anything? Give you any idea of why he was leaving early, where he was going?"

"Said he was almost finished with his business. That's all."

Almost finished with his business. Planning something new, and soon. More acid-slinging with a human target this time? He wouldn't do it in broad daylight, he wasn't that crazy. When and where? And where was he now?

Time to talk to Lieutenant St. John. But when Runyon got to the Los Alegres PD, he found that St. John was out on police business and not expected back until five thirty. He left a message, asking the lieutenant to wait if he came in early—the Henderson case, urgent.

Cliff Henderson wasn't at the west-side home construction site. Nobody was; work had been shut down for

the day. Runyon drove downtown to the Henderson Construction offices in a newish building along the west bank
of the Los Alegres River. The offices were open, but
Henderson wasn't there, either. He'd checked in and then
left about half an hour ago, the woman at the desk said.
Might find him the Oasis Bar; he and some members of his
crew often gathered there for a drink or two after work.

The Oasis had been operating for a lot of years in the
same location on the main drag. Somebody's house once,
judging by the architectural style, long ago converted into
a tavern and bedecked with neon signs. Old-fashioned inside, too: long bar, cracked leather booths, pool table,
jukebox, animal heads mounted on the walls, business
cards and dollar bills thumbtacked to the low ceiling. Guy
hangout. Runyon got the usual once-over locals give
strangers who walk in. The bar stools and booths were all
full, but it didn't take him long to spot Cliff Henderson—
crowded into a booth with three other guys, working on
pints of draft beer.

He moved over near the bar, stood there until he caught
Henderson's eye and then gestured to him. Henderson
didn't waste any time joining him. Runyon said, "Talk outside where it's private," and led the way through a rear door
into a parking lot dominated by pickups and motorcycles.

Henderson listened with no expression other than a
tightening of his facial muscles. When Runyon finished
talking he said, "I never heard of anybody named Tucker
Devries. Who the hell is he?"

"Disturbed personality with a perceived grudge against
the Henderson family."

"What kind of grudge, for Christ's sake?"

Irresponsible and unkind to lay the burden of Jenny Noakes's and his father's infidelity on Henderson's shoulders just yet. Runyon said only, "Details are still a little hazy."

"But you're saying it has something to do with my father."

"I'm afraid so."

Henderson shook his head, rubbed stubby fingers over the bristles on his jaw. "Five years since he passed away. What set Devries off after all this time?"

"That'll come out when he's in custody."

"You're sure he's the one?"

"He fits the profile, he's got a history of mental problems, and he's been in the area off and on since the trouble started."

"The cops know about this yet?"

"I'm seeing Lieutenant St. John in a few minutes. But the law demands hard proof and I don't have a lot of it to offer."

"So what, then? They won't arrest Devries right away?"

"Maybe not. They'll have to find him first."

"Yeah, that figures. And meanwhile, he's liable to make another move against Damon or me. You think he's crazy enough to use acid on one of us?"

"I wouldn't rule it out, Mr. Henderson."

"Miserable son of a bitch . . ."

"He drives a fifteen-year-old Dodge Caravan, white, no markings." Runyon recited the license number. "Pass that information on to your brother and your families. If you spot him anywhere, any time, call the police. Don't try to play it any other way."

"I'm not the hero type," Henderson said. "But I'll tell you one thing. I'm not about to hide in my house until they catch him, acid or no acid. I can't live scared. I damn well won't let him do that to me, either."

The talk with St. John went about the way Runyon expected it would. Skepticism, and a faint defensive irritation that a private investigator had managed to turn up information in three days that had eluded his department for three weeks.

"Listen, Runyon, I knew Lloyd Henderson personally for a lot of years. You'll never convince me he had anything to do with the murder of some young woman in Mendocino County."

"I'm not trying to," Runyon said. "It's Devries who believes it."

"Because of something of his mother's that's been hidden away for twenty years."

"Something in that trunk, yes."

"Such as what?"

"Whatever it is, it set him off, pushed him over the edge. Lloyd Henderson's no longer alive and desecrating his grave wasn't enough revenge for him."

"A goddamn psycho."

"The deadly kind. You knew all along that's what you were dealing with. We both did."

"Yeah. Yeah."

"So what're you going to do?"

"What do you expect me to do?"

"Put out an APB or at least a BOLO. He's still in the area."

"On your say-so? Just like that?" But St. John was chewing on it now, pinch-mouthed, like a dog with a new bone that tasted bad.

"For the Henderson brothers' sake, not mine."

"You already tell them about Devries?"

"Cliff Henderson, little while ago. He's our client—obligation to him as well as to the law. But I didn't say anything about Jenny Noakes. Not without corroboration."

"Well, that's something, anyway. All right. We'll look into it."

"Hard and fast, Lieutenant."

"You don't have to tell me my job," St. John said. He slapped his desktop, not too hard, for emphasis. "If you're right about this Devries character, we'll find him before he hurts anybody else."

One of those meaningless promises cops hand out to victims' families, the media, other civilians. Runyon didn't try to push it. Wouldn't have done any good. The lieutenant was all through listening to him.

Nothing more for Runyon in Los Alegres. He'd done his job, done his duty. Up to the authorities now. Like it or not, he was out of it.

22

I've been beating my head against this Cullrane murder all day long," I said to Kerry that night after dinner, "and all I've got for the effort is a headache."

"Well, I hate to say it, but that could be because you're trying to build a case where none exists."

"I don't think so. Angelina Pollexfen could be guilty, sure, and the shooting could've happened the way Yin and Davis have it figured, but there're too many inconsistencies— Pollexfen gathering her and Cullrane together in the library, feeding them drinks that were almost certainly drugged. The three-hour time lapse. The doors apparently being bolted from the inside for no good reason. Plus the kind of man Pollexfen is, plus the blackmail and revenge motives."

We were in our mom-and-pop chairs in the living room, a wood fire going, cups of espresso on the table between us. Emily was there, too, sitting cross-legged on the floor in front of the couch, reading *Pride and Prejudice* for her school English class. Behind her, Shameless lay draped half on the couch and half on her shoulder in one of his typical cat poses, purring loud enough to override the crackle of the fire. Entire family in after-dinner repose, everybody comfortable except me.

"There's a wrongness about the crime scene, too," I said. "I was in the library only three or four minutes, but I must've picked up on something because it didn't feel right afterward, still doesn't feel right."

"In what way?"

"Well, for one thing, it seemed staged. The more I think about it, the more everything about the case seems staged."

"The missing first editions, too, you mean?"

"Yes. All part of the same plan."

"So you're saying Pollexfen took the books?"

"More likely him than anybody else."

"Why would he do that?"

"Start the ball rolling. Set up a motive for his wife to kill her brother."

"But the murder method . . . that's what doesn't make sense."

"It will if I can figure out the how and the why. How do you arrange a shooting inside a locked room so you have a perfect alibi when it happens? And why use a shotgun, a weapon that makes a hell of a mess? Most of the carnage was confined to the fireplace, but there were blood spatters on some of the book spines. As passionate as Pollexfen is about his collection, why risk the damage?"

"Maybe he didn't realize how much of a mess there'd be."

"He's too smart to overlook something like that."

"The shotgun was the only weapon in the library?"

"The only gun in the house. Kept loaded and prominently displayed."

"Then it must've been a necessary part of whatever the trick was."

"Sure. But a big, heavy piece like that . . . cumbersome, impossible to gimmick."

Kerry sipped her espresso. "Is it possible Pollexfen shot Cullrane *before* he left for the auction? Recorded the sound of the shot, say, and set a timer so it played when it did?"

"Good theory, but no, that's not the answer." I glanced over at Emily and lowered my voice. "The room stank of burned powder and all the blood and gore was fresh. The shot we heard in the hallway is the one that killed Cullrane, no doubt of that."

"Well, then, I'm totally baffled. I can't imagine any other explanation."

"Neither can I. But there has to be one. He staged it all, right down to handing me his key so I'd be the one to unlock the two dead holts. And with precision timing."

"Are you certain the timing was so precise?"

"What do you mean?"

"Well, it seems incredible that he could arrange the shooting to the exact moment you and his secretary were in the house with him. How could he know he'd arrive home exactly when he did? He might've gotten stuck in traffic driving back from downtown."

I rattled that around inside my head. "You're right," I said. "The shooting didn't have to be perfectly timed. For that matter, Pollexfen didn't have to've been in the house at all for the plan to work."

"Just luck he was there when it happened?"

"From his point of view. Cullrane could already have been dead when Brenda Koehler and I came in. All Pollexfen really needed was a couple of witnesses to testify to the fact that the library door was locked. But that still doesn't help explain how he managed the shooting."

"There's another thing I don't understand," Kerry said. "Why would he devise such an elaborate scheme in the first place? I mean, if you're going to kill one person and frame another, why do it in such a complicated way?"

"Give himself a perfect alibi."

"Still. It seems so . . . overblown."

"Yes, it does. Bothers me, too, but—"

"Maybe he did it that way because he wanted to fool you, Dad." Emily, from her cross-legged slouch on the carpet.

Kerry said, "Emily, you're supposed to be reading, not eavesdropping on adult conversation."

I said, "No, wait a minute. What did you mean, maybe he did it to fool me?"

"You and the police," Emily said. "You said he collects mysteries and he's a big fan. What if he worked out a puzzle he thought nobody could solve, like in Agatha Christie's books? Only instead of writing it, he actually did it because he thinks he's smarter than real-life detectives."

Well, by God, I thought. My thirteen-year-old logical-minded, casually brilliant daughter.

Out of the mouths of babes.

I couldn't sleep. Cullrane's murder, the elusive wrongness of the crime scene, the gimmick that I couldn't quite figure out. And Emily's insight into Pollexfen's motives, which I should have realized on my own. Cullrane had as much as presented me with the same insight on Tuesday: *He's a schemer, you're a private eye. If you're smarter than he is, you'll figure it out like Mickey Spillane.*

Pollexfen, the mystery buff. Pollexfen, the sly manipulator. Completely in character for him to have devised what he considered a perfect crime and then to set it into motion, not only as revenge against two people he hated but as a match of his wits against those of trained investigators. It would explain the "stolen" first editions, the report to the police, the insurance claim—all part and parcel of a twisted and deadly game. Hell, he'd even thrown out little clues. His request to Barney Rivera that Great Western assign its best investigator to the case. Quoting the Sherlock Holmes dictum to me. A goddamn open challenge.

Yes, but what about the time element? Cullrane had been blackmailing him for a long time; he'd hated his wife for a long time. Waiting until he figured out the right gimmick? One factor, probably, but there had to be another—a trigger of some kind, the final push across the line between intellectual game and actual murder.

Something Cullrane had done, maybe an increased demand for money? Possibly. The poor state of Pollexfen's health? More likely. His age, his heart condition, those increased insurance premiums. Say he'd been told or intuited that he didn't have long to live. So why not go out in an egocentric blaze of glory, one suited to his intelligence, his passion for crime fiction, the nature of his victims, his penchant for manipulation. End his life basking in the glow of his cleverness and final triumph. Also perfectly in character.

Well, that wasn't going to happen. Not if I could help it.

How to prove his guilt to the police? Everything I had so far was circumstantial or speculative. They wouldn't listen unless I could offer some proof, or at least a plausible explanation of how the murder was committed.

What *was* it about the library, the crime scene, that had struck me as wrong? Concentrate. I visualized the room again, replayed in stop time the few minutes I'd spent in there.

The shotgun in relation to Cullrane's body?

No.

The position of the body?

. . . Yes, but that wasn't all of it.

Angelina Pollexfen's position?

No.

What then? Something else, something else . . .

The books.

The stack on the couch. And the blood-spattered rows next to the fireplace.

Yes, dammit, the books!

23

TUCKER DEVRIES

He hated bowling alleys.

Too many people crowded into a confined space on these league nights. And the noise—too much noise. Hard rubber and plastic balls racketing on polyurethane lanes and metal returns. Pins crashing, crashing, crashing. Yells, loud voices, loud laughter. An unending din that set up a pounding in his head until he felt like screaming.

They were unclean places, too. This one had sticky table-tops, soiled booth cushions and banquette seats, stained carpets. Dirt everywhere. He had to get up and go into the men's room every few minutes to scrub his hands and face. Not that it did much good. The filth had crept into his pores, making his skin crawl. The only way to completely cleanse himself was to stand under a hot shower, lather his body over and over with rough-textured soap, and it would be many hours before he could do that.

Tonight, though, the feeling of contamination was more

tolerable than on the other Thursday nights he'd come here
to Los Alegres Lanes. He felt too good otherwise. Excited,
but in that tamped-down, controlled way. Ready for the
first execution, with the second soon to come.

He watched Cliff Henderson step up to the ball return,
heft a gaudy, marbled blue ball in his big hands, then hook
it powerfully down the lane. Strike. Henderson's team-
mates cheered, made raucous comments, slapped his back.
Ninth frame of the third game and they were winning this
one as they'd won the previous two.

Now.

Devries got up from the banquette seat, walked to the
bathroom to rewash his hands and face. Straight outside
then and around to the north side of the building. He'd
parked the van there because it was a semideserted area,
not as well lighted as the big lot out front, crowded with
thick shadows created by a low bluff that flanked the
property on that side.

He unlocked the rear doors first, not hurrying, he had
plenty of time; keyed the driver's door open and leaned inside. From the glove compartment he transferred the roll
of duct tape to his left jacket pocket, then the gun he'd
bought to the right one. A .45 automatic, lightweight on
an aluminum frame but bulky—it made a bulge in the
pocket. That was why he'd kept it in the van until now.
Careful.

He left the van unlocked, walked back into the lobby to
the long front desk—keeping his right hand in his pocket,
around the gun, to minimize the bulge. From there he
could see that Henderson's team was done bowling. Chat-

tering among themselves now while they changed their shoes and bagged their balls. The first time he'd come here, before the cemetery burning, Henderson and his teammates had had drinks together in the bar. The other two times, aware that he was being stalked, Henderson had left immediately and gone home. That was what he'd do tonight. Creature of habit. Couldn't give up his twice-weekly league bowling, the only recreation he indulged in regularly. He was cautious, wary, but that wouldn't matter. Surprise, Cliff — surprise!

Henderson putting his jacket on was the signal to move. Devries turned away from the desk, walking casually, and went outside again and down the row in the front lot to where Henderson's pickup was slotted. An SUV stood next to it. A man getting into his car two rows away was the only person in sight.

Devries moved around to the side of the SUV, to where he had a clear vantage point. Unzipped the jacket pocket, got a tight grip on the gun. All set.

He watched the entrance. Brightly lit, gradations of grainy black on both sides, pole lights throwing glints of light off metal and glass. Perfect composition for a night study. Too bad he didn't have time to set up a shot with his Nikkormat or even the Kodak digital. But there'd be plenty of time to create other mementos, much better ones, later on.

After two minutes Henderson came out alone, lugging his bowling bag. Devries ducked down out of sight. Footsteps in the cold darkness, coming close. The sound of the heavy bag thumping into the back of the pickup. He was moving by then, soundlessly, the gun out and ready. Timed it perfectly. Henderson was unlocking the driver's door, his back turned. Heard him coming but not soon enough to react.

Devries used his body to crowd Henderson against the door, jabbing the automatic hard into his rib cage, saying in a low voice close to his ear, "This is a gun. Move and I'll shoot you dead. Promise."

He could feel the sudden tension in Henderson's body, the tight coiling of muscles. Heard him say, "You," in a voice that sounded more angry than scared. Well, that would change. Oh, yes, it would.

"Start walking, Cliff."

"You bastard, you won't get away with this—"

Devries dug the barrel into his ribs, hard enough to make him grunt. "Walk, I said. Or you'll never walk again."

". . . Where?"

"North side of the building. Cut through the rows away from the lights. If anybody comes out before we get there, don't stop or slow down. We're just a couple of buddies on the move."

"What're you going to do?" Still angry, but scared enough of the gun not to try any heroics.

"You'll find out. Walk!"

Henderson walked. Jerkily, at first, then at a more even pace. Devries stayed in close, holding on to the sleeve of Henderson's jacket with his left hand so he could keep the automatic's muzzle tight against the ribs. Nobody showed before they reached the corner, went ahead into the shadows.

At the rear of the van he jerked Henderson to a stop. "Listen. Step ahead a couple of paces. Don't turn around."

Henderson obeyed. In the cold stillness, the sound of his breathing was loud, raspy. Vapor came out of his mouth in hard little puffs, like tobacco smoke.

Devries started to open the rear door. Voices stopped him—two bowlers with bags, yakking to each other, heading around the corner toward them. He said, quick and low, "Move or make a sound, I'll kill you." Henderson looked over his shoulder, but that was all he did.

Devries shifted position so he could watch the two men and Henderson at the same time. Neither bowler paid any attention to them. They deposited their bags in the backseat of a car parked up near the front of the lot, got in. The engine rumbled, exhaust spumed out, backup lights flashed. If they came this way . . . But they didn't. The driver backed around sharply, so that the headlights splashed out in the other direction, and the car rattled off through the main lot.

Quickly Devries opened the van's rear door. Dark inside; he'd unscrewed the bulb. "Back up two steps," he said to Henderson. "Then get in and lie on your belly, head toward the front."

"You son of a bitch, I'm not going to—"

"Inside."

"Whatever you're planning, you won't get away with it. The police know who you are."

"Shut up and get inside. Last time I'll say it. If you don't, I'll shoot you and put you in dead. Don't think I don't mean it."

Henderson made a low, growling sound, but he backed up, hunched a little now, and turned sideways and looked into the dark interior as if he were looking into a pit. The sound came out of him again.

"Hurry up! Facedown, feet together, hands behind you."

Henderson did as he was told. Squirmed on the mat, breathing heavily as he brought both arms around behind him.

"Where're you taking me?" Voice muffled against the carpet mat.

Devries said, "You'll find out," and went to work with the roll of duct tape.

24

I dreamed the answer to the locked-room trick.

Feed your subconscious enough data and set it to work on a problem before you go to sleep, and sometimes you'll wake up with the solution. That had happened to me before, but this was the first time my subconscious had kicked one up in a jumble of sleep images and metaphor.

In my dream I was in Gregory Pollexfen's brightly lit library. Others were there, too, Pollexfen and his wife and Jeremy Cullrane, and I seemed to be watching them from an elevated position, as if from the top of one of the bookshelf ladders. At first I couldn't tell what was going on, but the longer I stared down the clearer the scene became. Then there was a sudden flash and a burst of silent noise, like you sometimes get in a dream, and all at once I was out of it and sitting up in bed wide awake, the images still clear and sharp.

I must have done some thrashing around or made an

involuntary sound because Kerry woke up and rolled over and said with groggy alarm, "What? What is it, what's the matter?"

"Got it," I said. "I know how it was done."

"How what was done?"

"The murder. How Pollexfen worked it—the only way it could've been done. Drugging the two of them, that's the key. Ingenious, simple—and as nasty as it gets. A sick new way of killing somebody. He can even pretend there's no blood on his hands because technically it's not a homicide at all."

"What're you talking about? How can a homicide not be a homicide?"

"When it's murder by suicide."

25

JAKE RUNYON

He was awake as soon as the bedside phone rang. Alert, with the receiver in his hand before a second ring. Product of self-training when he was on the Seattle PD, so any late-night calls wouldn't disturb Colleen.

The digital clock on the nightstand read 2:29. He registered that before he said, "Runyon."

"I know it's late, Mr. Runyon, I'm sorry to be calling so late, but I've been half out of my mind." Woman's voice, distraught, breathless. Tracy Henderson. "The police, Lieutenant St. John, they don't seem able to do anything and I thought you might have some idea—"

"Slow down, Mrs. Henderson. What's happened?"

"It's Cliff. He . . . oh God, he went to bowl in his league tonight like he does every Thursday. I begged him not to, I begged him to stay home, but he said he'd be with people, friends, nothing could happen—"

"Slow," Runyon said again.

Stuttery inhale, whistling exhale. "He didn't come home. I called the police when he wasn't here by eleven and they . . . his truck was still at the lanes but they can't find him anywhere."

"Last seen when?"

"Right after he finished bowling. He told his team-mates he was going straight home."

"What time was that?"

"Quarter of ten."

"Was there anything wrong with the truck?" Acid, he was thinking, but he didn't want to use the word.

"No, it was just parked there, unlocked. Cliff wouldn't have left it like that, he always locks it, always. His bag and ball were in the back."

Caught by surprise as he was about to get into the pickup. Hurt in some way? Possibly, but not with any weapon that would cause noise, bring attention.

"I don't understand," Mrs. Henderson said. Sobs in her voice; she was on the ragged edge of hysteria. "All those other terrible things that madman Devries did, the attack on Damon, and now this . . ."

Escalation, sure, but not the expected kind. Kidnapping instead of hit-and-run assault. Change in Devries's pattern. Why?

He said, "The police know about Devries, the kind of vehicle he drives—"

"A white Dodge van, yes, Cliff told me. Lieutenant St. John said he already knew about it from you."

"Did he put out an APB on Devries and the van?"

"APB? I don't . . ."

"All points bulletin. To police agencies statewide."

"I don't know, he didn't say anything about that."

Maybe St. John had, maybe he hadn't. He was the extra-cautious type. Even if Henderson's sudden disappearance had convinced him that Devries was the perp, it might be too late.

"I asked him what they were doing," she said, "but all he'd say was everything possible, everything possible. What does that *mean*?"

It didn't mean anything. Copspeak. Synonym for frustration and lack of clear direction. Whatever Runyon could say would be more of the same, so he left her question unanswered.

"Why would Devries kidnap Cliff? Where would he take him?"

The cemetery was one possibility. Put the son down with the father, burn him the way he'd burned Lloyd Henderson's ashes. But Cliff was only one son. Devries was after both.

Runyon said, "Have you talked to Damon?"

"Yes, before the lieutenant came and again afterward."

"He and his family all right? No trouble at their home?"

"No, they're fine. Cliff . . . only Cliff . . ."

One at a time, then, rather than both brothers together. The cemetery was definitely out. Besides, St. John would have had the same line of thought, ordered the cemetery checked out first thing; he was cautious and defensive and hard to convince, but he was no dummy.

"Where?" Mrs. Henderson said again. "Why? What does he want with Cliff?"

To kill him. Maybe torture him with acid first. It had reached that point. Psychos were unpredictable for the most part, but an escalation of a monomaniacal psychosis like Devries's was something you could calculate with reasonable certainty.

"I don't know," he lied.

"Is there anything you can do, Mr. Runyon? You've done so much for us already, I hate to ask any more of you, but I feel so helpless. . . ."

What could he do? Talk to St. John, and if an APB hadn't been put out on Devries and the Dodge van, try again to persuade him? St. John wouldn't like that. Further infringement on his territory. It was even possible he'd dislike the interference enough to make trouble with the state licensing board.

"Anything? Please?"

Begging him now. He couldn't say no. Couldn't put her off, either. The hell with St. John and the possible consequences.

Right back in it, like it or not.

"I'll drive up," he said, "talk to St. John."

"When?"

"As soon as I can." He wouldn't be able to sleep anymore, and he couldn't lie in bed or rattle around the apartment until dawn waiting for news. The restlessness, the need for movement, was already sharp in him. "If you have any word about your husband before I contact you, call me on my cell phone."

"Yes, I will. Thank you, Mr. Runyon. Thank you!"

For nothing, probably. Except wasted effort.

He put the teakettle on, showered in cold water to get the grit out of his eyes and sharpen his mind. Two quick cups of tea helped, too. He'd never needed much sleep. Four hours, which was about what he'd gotten tonight, was enough for him to function normally.

Out of the apartment, through the mostly empty late-night streets, across the fog-cloaked span of the Golden Gate Bridge.

Why the change in Devries's pattern? Acid in all the other attacks except for the one on Damon Henderson, but the blows with the tire iron had been the result of circumstance, not planning. What was he up to this time?

Through the MacArthur tunnel, down the winding expanse of Waldo Grade.

Where would he take Henderson? Not somewhere in or close to Los Alegres, that didn't fit Devries's profile or motives.

Where?

26

TUCKER DEVRIES

He adjusted the focus on his Nikkormat, checked the light meter, made another adjustment. The dawn light coming through the broken window and open door was just right—kind of pearly, like an oyster shell. But it wasn't strong enough yet—he'd still have to use the Vivitar flash. Better try to make these last few snaps as perfect as he could.

This was the second roll of film he'd shot. The first roll, last night after they got here, had been all handheld with little or no light—a dozen pix in and out of the van, the rest in here. No way to know how well they'd turn out until he developed them, but he was good at estimating distances and exposure needs under those conditions; he had a feeling they'd be pretty good. This second roll he *knew* would be good. As soon as it was daylight he'd carried the tripod in and set the Nikkormat up on it. Every shot since had been calculated, meticulously framed and lighted.

One more adjustment. Okay, ready. No, not just yet. When he squinted through the viewfinder, his vision was a little smeary. Lack of sleep. Twenty-four hours without it now and he was bone-tired. But there was still a lot to do. He'd sleep when he was done. He'd sleep real good then.

He wiped his eye on his jacket sleeve. It still felt sticky with mucus. Henderson was watching him. Well, let him watch, let him wait, he wasn't going anywhere with two rolls of duct tape around him and the big wooden chair.

Devries went outside into the chill morning hush, then around the cabin to the stream that ran murmuring along the edge of the woods. The water was so cold it made him shudder, numbed his hands and cheeks. But clean, sweet, free of pollutants. So much better than city water. His vision was clear when he finished, and his skin tingled.

Inside the cabin again, he dried off on the towel from the van. Now he was ready. He rechecked the light meter, took another squint through the viewfinder. Henderson was framed in the exact center. Red eyes, cracked lips, gray-flecked beard stubble, animal scowl. Perfect.

"Smile," he said.

"Fuck you."

Henderson had said that before, at least a dozen times since he'd dragged him in here from the van. Didn't bother Devries. He'd expected whining, begging, but all he'd gotten so far was anger and abuse. Give the devil's spawn his due. Henderson had plenty of guts. He wouldn't die screaming, the way Mother must have. The way Lloyd Henderson should have.

Okay, set up another shot. Use the timer this time, so

he could be in it, too. He'd taken a few of those two-shots before, but one more wouldn't hurt. The gun to Henderson's head again? The closed jar of acid tilted above his face? No, something different. Maybe open the jar, dribble a little of the acid on Henderson's leg, capture the vapor from sizzling flesh and what was sure to be an open-mouthed yell of pain? No, the pain would make him thrash around and spoil the shot. Save the acid for later, when Henderson was dead. Burn what was left of him, the way he'd burned the father's ashes.

Make it the gun again, then, only from another perspective. Kneel down behind him, tuck the muzzle up under his throat. Good! The composition would be just right.

The automatic was on the table by the door, with his camera bag and briefcase. When he had the camera ready, he went and got the gun and thumbed off the safety. Henderson watched him with his hard, fearless eyes.

"You going to finish it now?"

"No. Sit still."

Devries set the timer for twenty seconds, went around behind Henderson and into the pose he'd decided on, smiling a little, not too much—a grim executioner's smile. Henderson moved his head and his eyes, the only parts of his body he could move, trussed up the way he was. It was so quiet inside and outside that the sound of the shutter tripping was like the pop of a small pistol.

"Why don't you just kill me and get it over with?"

Henderson had said that before, too. Devries gave back the same answer as he got to his feet: "Not yet."

"Sadistic son of a bitch."

"I'm not sadistic."

"Hell you're not. All those pictures, keeping me wrapped up like a goddamn mummy, torturing me."

"Torture? I haven't hurt you, have I?"

"Making me wait before you kill me. Like a fucking terrorist."

"No! Executioner."

"Bullshit, man. How many times do I have to tell you my father didn't kill your mother?"

"The evidence says he did. Evidence doesn't lie."

"Evidence. Christ."

"Her own words, her own testimony."

"I don't care what she wrote in her diary or whatever it is. He didn't kill her. He never hurt anyone in his life."

"You want me to read it to you again? All the evidence?"

"No."

"Yes."

He went and got the notebook from his briefcase, handling it carefully as he always did. Not a diary or a journal, just a random collection of notes Mother had made—dates, names, events, impressions, reminders. He was in there, many times until the last few pages. "My sweet baby, Tucker. My handsome boy, Tucker." His miserable damn father a few times, the sentences bitter and angry. Men she'd dated, casual affairs, you couldn't blame her for seeking love and comfort after Anthony Noakes abandoned the two of them. And then Lloyd Henderson. Nine entries, right at the end, five happy and hopeful, three infuriating and terrible. Evidence. Irrefutable testimony.

The notebook opened in his hands, as if by itself, to that last section. Mother's round, cramped handwriting in faded purple ink. The smeared word at the bottom of the last page: teardrop, tearstain. Mother's tears.

He stood next to Henderson, loomed over him, and read the passages aloud again, the same ones in the same order.

" 'I love Lloyd. More than I ever loved Anthony. I know he's married and he's never made any promises, never said he loves me, but I feel his love when we're in bed. It's not just sex. He loves me as much as I love him.'

" 'Went to his camp today, I just needed to see him for a few minutes. But I shouldn't have. He was there with his friends and he made me leave. He was so angry, like Anthony used to get sometimes. It's a side to Lloyd I hope I never see again.'

" 'I'm going to have Lloyd's baby. Our love child. I didn't do it on purpose, it was an accident, but he'll be happy when I tell him. I know he will.'

" 'He was furious, that awful angry side of him. He said the baby's not his. He said he doesn't want to see me anymore, it's over between us. How can he say that after what we've been to each other?'

" 'I drove down to Los Alegres, I saw his wife, I saw him at his office. He called me a dirty little slut. He said he'd kill me if I told anybody he was the father of my baby. The way he looked at me . . . like he really did want me dead. God, how could I have been so stupid?' "

And the last entry, the final damning piece of testimony, written the day before she disappeared. " 'Lloyd drove up this afternoon alone. I saw his truck go by the store. After work tomorrow I'm going to his camp. I don't care if he doesn't want me, he has to help me with the baby. He has to. He used me and now he has to pay. I'll make him pay.' "

Devries closed the notebook. His eyes were wet again, like hers were when she wrote those last words. "You see?" he said. "You see? She didn't make him pay, he made her pay. That night, right here. Her and the baby both. Strangled her and then dumped her in the woods for the animals . . . the animals . . ."

"It wasn't my father. She wasn't killed here."

"She was. I know she was."

"Somebody else . . ."

"That same night? Attacked her, strangled her, that same night? Coincidence? No, Henderson. No, no, no!"

"I'll never believe my father did it. He had an affair with your mother; all right, he wasn't a saint. But he wasn't a murderer, either."

"He was! He's dead, I can't punish him, but I've got you and I'll get your brother, too, devil's sons, bastards, you'll both die in his place, right here where he killed my mother and my baby brother or sister!"

He realized he was screaming. His temples were pounding, his face was hot and running sweat. Control. Don't lose it now, it's not finished yet, there's still the other one, Damon. Take deep breaths. Get a grip.

"Go ahead then," Henderson said. "Shoot me, get it over with."

"No."

"Do it, damn you."

"No. Not yet."

Now he felt dirty all over. Crawly, as if bugs had come up out of the floor, dropped off the ceiling, and were trying to burrow beneath his skin. Scrub them off, get clean for the execution. You had to be clean. For Mother's sake. She'd drummed that into his head so many times. Be clean, Tucker. Always keep yourself *clean.*

He went outside, stood sucking in the chill mountain air until it cooled him and his head quit pounding. He made himself walk slowly around the cabin to the stream. When he knelt down on the bank, he realized he was still holding the gun; he put the safety on, shoved the automatic inside his belt. In the splashes and scrubs of icy water, the bugs shriveled and died and his skin tingled and he was clean again. He stood, dripping, and went around the front of the cabin.

A man was standing there against the front wall.

Devries stopped, staring in disbelief. At first he thought he must be hallucinating. But no, no, the man was real. Big, hard-looking, somebody he'd never seen before.

"Hello, Tucker."

He reached for the gun, his fingers, still wet, slip-sliding around the handle. But the stranger was already moving, fast. There was a slash of pain at the joining of his neck and shoulder and the entire right side of his body went numb. He stood there bent and swaying, confused. Left hand, get the gun with his left hand . . . but the gun wasn't there anymore, the stranger had it now.

Another cut of pain, all through his left side this time.

And all at once he was down on the grass, writhing, numb all over, looking up at the hard face above him through a watery blur. He tried to say something, he wasn't even sure what it was, but his throat muscles wouldn't work. The noises he made sounded like a baby's gurgle.

The man caught hold of his jacket collar and he felt himself being dragged through the dew-wet grass, pulled up the porch steps, slammed back against a support post. He couldn't prevent any of it, couldn't move his arms, could barely feel his legs. Paralyzed. *What did he do to me?*

Something cold and hard snapped around one wrist. Through the blur he saw that it was a ring of steel. Handcuff. The other ring clicked around a railing post. Hard footsteps thudded in his ears, across the porch, into the cabin. Voices, then, like noisy fish swimming in the confusion inside his head.

"Runyon! My God, I'd given up hope—"

"You all right? He hurt you, burn you?"

"No, no. Just numb, cramped . . . Where's Devries?"

"Handcuffed outside."

"How did you—?"

"Judo. He won't give us any trouble."

Sounds of tape being torn loose. And the voices, still swimming.

"I thought for sure I was dead. How'd you know where he took me?"

"I was here before, three days ago. Figured it out when I remembered the chair and the table over there, the only things he hadn't wrecked and burned. I had to park down the road so he wouldn't hear me coming. Wasn't sure I'd make it in time."

"You almost didn't. He's crazy . . . he thinks my father killed his mother. It's not true. I don't care what kind of proof he thinks he's got."

It is true, Devries thought. It is, *it is*. Lloyd Henderson. Dead, and his sons both alive. I'm sorry, Mother. I tried. For you and the baby. I tried so hard but I waited too long.

Tears in his eyes, deepening the blur. Like her tears that last night, the droplet on the smeared purple ink.

He felt dirty. He felt as if now, no matter what he did, he would never be clean again.

27

Inspectors Yin and Davis weren't particularly happy to see me—at first.

It was a quarter past eight and they'd just come on duty. They were having coffee at Yin's desk, talking over something she'd pulled up on her computer screen. The coffee smelled good—I'd had a quick cup before leaving home and was ready for another—but neither of them offered me any.

"You again," Davis said. "What is it this time?"

"Some things you're going to want to hear. Question first. Have you given Gregory Pollexfen permission to clean up his library yet?"

"Later this morning. Get him off our backs about it."

"So you've still got both keys."

Yin said, "We've got them. Why?"

"He killed Jeremy Cullrane," I said. "I'm pretty sure I know how and why, and I think I can prove it to you."

They looked at me, looked at each other, looked at me again. Cop looks: poker-faced skepticism.

"Give me half an hour in the library, then a few more minutes with Pollexfen. Both of you present, of course. That's all I ask."

"You say you can prove he killed Cullrane," Yin said. "While he was with you outside in the hallway."

"That's right."

"Okay, let's hear your theory."

I told them how I had it figured. Method, motives, and what I expected to find in the library. They listened without interruption. When I was done, they weren't skeptical anymore. Davis said to his partner, "You know, it could've been managed that way. Explains why Pollexfen's been so anxious to get into the library. It's a better fit, too. No inconsistencies."

"We'll find out," Yin said. "Call the man and tell him we're on our way with his keys."

Pollexfen was in a bright, almost smug mood—at first. He must have been surprised to see me with the two inspectors and the patrolman they'd brought along, but he didn't show it. Still convinced he'd outsmarted and bamboozled everybody concerned. It wasn't until Yin told him she and Davis and I would be spending some time alone in the library that you could see the arrogance fade a little and the worm of doubt wiggle in.

"What for?" he said. "You've already examined the room, you and your forensics experts."

Yin said, "Some things we want to check on."

"What things? What are you looking for?"

"We'll tell you after we're done."

"I demand to be present. It's my library, my house—"

"We'd rather you wait in the living room, Mr. Pollexfen."

Blood-rush darkened his face; he bounced the ferrule of his cane hard on the floor. "By God, your superiors will hear about this!"

Yin ignored that. She directed the patrolman to stay with Pollexfen, and the three of us went down the hallway to the library. The yellow crime scene tape was in place over the door, the police seal and both bolt locks secure. Yin removed the tape, broke the seal, keyed us in. Davis put on the lights.

The air in there had a stale quality, a faint residue of Wednesday's violence. Anyone who thinks the odor of death doesn't linger in a closed space has never been in one. It can and does—for days, even weeks. And you don't need to be extra sensitive to be aware of it.

This was my show; Yin and Davis stood off, waiting for my lead. I took a long look around, picturing the room as I'd first seen it after the shooting. The eight books were still on the couch, but the stack wasn't quite as orderly; the inspectors or the techs must have moved them. The same book was still on top, though. The dried mess inside the fireplace had been sampled and dusted and sprayed— the techs again. In the rows of bookshelves alongside, the blood spatters shone dark and crusty, like rust spots, on the Mylar jacket protectors.

I went to those shelves first, donning the pair of white latex gloves Yin had given me, and spent a few minutes examining the authors and titles in the affected rows on each side. "The first time Pollexfen showed me around in here," I said, "every book was arranged in alphabetical order by the author's last name. The books on these two shelves were *N, O,* and part of *P.* Look at them now."

Yin and Davis looked. "Out of order," she said. "Some *K*'s, *L*'s, other letters mixed in."

"You'll have to take my word on this, but none of the replacements are particularly valuable. There's only one reason a meticulous collector like Pollexfen would've switched the books around."

Davis said, "Get the valuable ones out of the way. Protect them from possible splatter damage."

"That's it. The same reason he arranged the killing so that most of the blood and gore ended up inside the fireplace. He cares more about his first editions than anything else. Once he decided to stage the murder in here, protecting the books that can't be easily replaced was his number-one priority."

I moved over to the stack on the couch, sat down beside it. The book on top, its Mylar cover coated with a fine film of fingerprint powder, was *The Talking Clock* by Frank Gruber. I'd noted that on Wednesday because Gruber had been a frequent contributor to the pulp magazines in the '30s and '40s and I'd read dozens of his stories, one of them *The Talking Clock* as a magazine serial. With a forefinger, I lifted the front cover and the first couple of pages. Fine condition, but no author signature or inscription.

I leaned down to look at the spines of the others in the

stack. Two were also by Gruber: *The Navy Colt* and *The Hungry Dog*. The rest: *Bodies Are Where You Find Them*, Brett Halliday. *Death on the Door Mat*, M. V. Heberden. *Vivanti*, Sydney Horler. *The Corpse at the Quill Club*, Amelia Reynolds Long. *The Mandarin's Sapphire*, Dwight Marfield.

"Eight more books," I said, "that we were supposed to think were targeted for theft by Cullrane. The first eight are ultrarare, some one-of-a-kind, the authors and titles recognizable to nonbibliophiles, and worth half a million on the collectors' market. But these eight are just the opposite— more or less obscure titles by relatively minor writers." I tapped the copy of *The Talking Clock*. "I looked this one up on the Internet. In fine condition, without an author inscription, it's worth a maximum of two hundred dollars. The others here by the same writer can't be worth any more. I don't know about the other five, but I'd be surprised if their value is even a thousand dollars combined."

Davis said, "Same purpose as the spatter rows. Protecting his valuables."

"Right. He figured I wouldn't notice and that no one on the investigating team would be enough of a bibliophile to tell the difference."

"That makes two marks against Mr. Pollexfen," Yin said.

Number three coming up: the eight stolen rarities.

Except that they hadn't been stolen at all. They were right here in this room and had been all along.

It took the three of us more than an hour to find all of them. I'd told the inspectors what to look for and it was

Yin who made the initial discovery, the inscribed first edition of Ellery Queen's *The Roman Hat Mystery*. I found the Doyle, Hammett's *The Maltese Falcon,* and Christie's *The Murder of Roger Ackroyd*; Davis the other Hammett and Chandler's *The Big Sleep*; and Yin, Rex Stout's *Fer-de-Lance* and the Cain.

They were scattered throughout the collection, among the *A*'s, the *E*'s, the *G*'s, the *R*'s, the *T*'s, the *V*'s, the *W*'s. Mostly on the higher shelves, so they'd be even less easy to spot. Not that there'd been much chance I or anybody else, even a fellow bibliophile, would have found them by accident or on a cursory inspection; you had to know what you were looking for, and you had to examine nearly all of the thousands of books in the library.

Such a simple trick—a neat little variation on Poe's "Purloined Letter." All Pollexfen had done was take off the original dust jackets, wrap the books in different jackets of the exact same size from titles by lesser authors, and set them back on the shelves with the lesser authors' other books. *The Maltese Falcon,* for instance, was hidden inside the jacket for *The Fires at Fitch's Folly* by Kenneth Whipple. After all eight were hidden, it was easy for Pollexfen to slip the rare dust jackets out of the library in a briefcase and hide them in a safe place. The books by Whipple and the others he'd used were right there on his desk in plain sight—unjacketed copies mixed in with jacketed ones that I'd noticed on my first visit and assumed were new acquisitions. To complete the illusion of theft, Pollexfen had left gaps in the shelves where the "missing" valuables had originally stood.

"Three marks against him," Yin said when we had all eight rarities. "You've been right on everything so far."

Davis said, "Let's go see if he's right about the rest of it."

Under the watchful eye of the patrolman, Pollexfen was stumping around the living room with the tip of his cane making hard, angry noises on the rug-covered tiles. He stopped when he saw the three of us come in, started to say something that didn't get out of his throat. It was the eight books I was carrying, spines outward, that checked him. His brows and his mouth pulled down into a bunched grimace.

"What have you got there?" he demanded. "How dare you remove books from my library without my permission?"

I said, "You should be glad to see these. Familiar even from where you're standing, aren't they?"

He came stumping toward me. "Give me those!"

I said, "No, you don't," and Davis stepped between Pollexfen and me to stop his advance. "They're evidence now."

"Evidence—bah! Where are the dust wrappers?"

"Wherever you hid them."

He waved that away. "The books—where did you find them?"

"Same answer. Where you hid them. Inside jackets by other authors, filed under those authors' names on the shelves."

Another dismissive wave. Brazen it out, that was his style. Contemptuously spin and deny and manipulate to the end. He'd've been right at home in the nation's capital.

"Is that what Jeremy did? Hid them right under my nose until he could find a way to remove them later on?"

"Your scheme, not his. One of several."

"Nonsense."

"Fact. Here's another: the eight books on the couch Cullrane was supposed to've gathered before he was shot. There's not a highly prized first edition among them."

"No? I told you he didn't know books, didn't I?"

"Then how did he happen to pick eight of the most valuable the first time around? Blind luck? No, you chose the second batch because you didn't want to risk damage to expensive books. The same reason you replaced expensive ones with inexpensive ones on the shelves alongside the fireplace."

He glared at me; there was hate in his eyes now, black as midnight. "I did no such thing. If books were moved around in there, Jeremy did it. Or Angelina."

"They'd have no reason to. Only you."

"Blatantly false accusations. You can't prove any of them."

"Except for felony insurance fraud," I said. "All the police need to prove that is the missing dust jackets. You wouldn't risk damage to the valuable ones, so they have to be some place secure. Your safe deposit box—that's a good bet."

A muscle twitched under his right eye. I'd made the right guess.

Yin saw it, too. She said, "All it'll take to find out is a search warrant."

"Before you can get one," Pollexfen said, "I'll withdraw my claim with Great Western Insurance. Then you'll have nothing criminal against me. A man can do what he wants with his own possessions if he's not committing a crime."

"Nothing against you?" I said. "Not committing a crime? Last time I checked, premeditated homicide was still a Class A felony."

"Homicide! Now what are you claiming?"

"That you killed your brother-in-law."

"That's preposterous. Angelina shot him, on purpose or accidentally—"

"No, she didn't. You. Just like all the rest of it—designed and carried out by you."

"That's insane. How could I have shot the man when I was with you and my secretary when it happened? The doors to the library were double-locked, you unlocked them yourself."

"We know how you did it," I said. "We also know why. Revenge, for one thing. You hated Cullrane because he was bleeding you over the illegalities in your Greenfield Aeronautics takeover. Hated your wife because of her infidelity. Kill him, frame her—double payback."

"Double nonsense," he said.

"But that wasn't enough for you. You had to do it in a way that satisfied your ego and your passion for crime fiction. Clever mastermind devises ingenious murder plot, then sets out to match wits with real-life detectives. The one thing you forgot is that the too-smart criminal almost always makes mistakes in his calculations, so he hardly ever gets away with his crimes. Life imitating art."

"You know what I think?" Pollexfen said. "I think you're full of shit."

I said to Yin, "Never fails. Back one of the moneyed class into a corner, the respectability peels off like dead skin."

"You haven't backed me anywhere."

"Pretty close, I'd say."

"Words—just a lot of meaningless words. You believe you know how I committed a mythical murder? Go ahead, explain it."

"Murder by suicide," I said.

The phrase jolted him. Until I said it he'd thought we were guessing, that we didn't actually know how the murder had been arranged. His arrogance, his sense of invincibility, was based on his conviction that he'd created an unsolvable puzzle. I'd blown up that assumption with three little words.

His mouth bent into a sneer, but he forced it and it didn't come off. "That makes no sense whatsoever."

"It's pretty simple, really. Like the rest of your plan. You gathered your wife and her brother into the library and fed them martinis laced with Klonopin—enough of the drug to knock them out for approximately three hours. You knew about the effects of clonazepam and alcohol because of the time your wife ended up in the hospital when she made the mistake of mixing the two. I don't know how you figured the exact dosage, but I can make a couple of guesses. Casual questions to a trusted doctor or chemist. Or more likely, by trial and error. You're not above feeding yourself the same cocktail and suffering through the aftereffects until you had the right mix and the right time frame."

He said nothing this time. The muscle twitched again under his eye.

"The way you set it up," I said, "Cullrane could have died before you got back from the auction, before Brenda Koehler and I were in the house. It was only important that he be found dead with your wife in a sealed room, and that you have an unshakable alibi for the time of death. You almost miscalculated; another two or three minutes and I might have gotten in there in time to save Cullrane's life. As it was, the fact that he died when he did, while the three of us were together in the hallway, must have seemed like a huge bonus to you.

"All right. Once Cullrane and Angelina were out cold, you pulled her off the couch and laid her on the floor next to the desk. You took eight not too expensive books off the shelves, probably at random, and stacked them on the couch. You put the second key, the one you had made from your own, into Cullrane's pocket and then dragged him over to the fireplace and stretched him out on his back with his head propped up against the hearth bricks. How am I doing so far?"

"Still full of shit."

"You took the shotgun down, made sure it was ready to fire, and laid it vertically on top of Cullrane's body with the butt wedged down between his knees and the barrels shoved inside his mouth. Then you wrapped his hands around the trigger guard, the fingers interlaced to hold them in place, both forefingers hooked together through the guard and tight on the trigger closest to his face. He was a tall man with long arms; the fit would have been just right. Then you walked out, double-locked the door with your own key, and left for the book auction.

"Death trap for an unconscious man. Clonazepam mixed with alcohol leaves a person groggy and disoriented when he starts to wake up. Cullrane did what anybody in that condition would when he felt his mouth clogged and tasted gunmetal: he struggled automatically to free his hands, pull the barrels out of his mouth. Instead, his laced fingers triggered the weapon and blew off the back of his head, and the recoil jerked it loose and threw it down over his legs. Murder by suicide."

"That's a crazy theory," Pollexfen said. "It wouldn't work."

"Sure it would, if it was set up properly by a person who knows guns. Ask Inspector Davis. He's a gun expert himself."

"It'd work, all right," Davis said, "if you lightened the trigger pull to less than four pounds. Which Ballistics says you did. Cold-blooded, man."

Pollexfen said, "Ridiculous speculation, that's all it is. You can't prove I did any of that."

Yin said, "Motive, opportunity, the drug evidence. Plus what we found in the library and the false insurance claim. That's enough for us."

"Go ahead, then, take me into custody. I'll sue the police department for false arrest."

"You couldn't make it stick," I said.

"You think the district attorney can make charges

against me stick? The case would never go to trial. Even if did, no jury would convict me."

"Maybe not, but then prosecutors and juries are both unpredictable. But let's say you hire a hotshot criminal attorney and he gets the case thrown out, or you're acquitted on reasonable doubt if it does go to trial. Either way you still lose, Pollexfen. You got rid of Cullrane, but the frame against Angelina's already fallen apart. She has her own hotshot attorney—he'll get the charges against her dropped, guaranteed. You lose the game, too—your perfect crime isn't perfect, it didn't even come close. The media will have a field day at your expense."

Got him where he lived, inside his massive ego, and it broke him. He growled, "You bastard!" and came at me swinging his cane. Davis caught it and yanked it out of his hand.

Yin said, "Like the man said, Mr. Pollexfen, life imitates art. People who think they're smarter than the law hardly ever get away with it."

Pollexfen had nothing more to say. He stood there marinating in his hate and his defeat while Davis handcuffed him and Yin read him his rights.

28

JAKE RUNYON

When he arrived to keep his Saturday night date with Bryn, she said she didn't feel like going out. "Would you mind if we just stayed here tonight? I've got salad fixings and a bottle of wine in the fridge."

"Whatever you like."

They ate in the dining room, surrounded by rosewood sideboards and glass-fronted cabinets she'd inherited from her parents. By candlelight, because it was pale and soft and she could hold her head so that the covered side of her face was shadowed. The scarf she wore was dark red with a black pattern of Chinese characters. A different one just for him?

There wasn't much conversation. She seemed far away tonight, even more so than usual. Not unhappy, not exactly pensive—just adrift deep within. He respected her need for solitude, as always, so he didn't try to make small talk. He wasn't good at it anyway. The Henderson case was still on his mind, but he wouldn't have discussed it with her if she'd asked. Even with Colleen, he'd never talked about his work. Professional life, private life—he believed in keeping them separate, so that the one wouldn't taint the other.

After dinner they took their wine into the lamplit living room. Bryn turned on the gas-log fire and then some music, something quiet by Brahms, and they sat in companionable silence with the hissing flames making flicker patterns on the walls and furniture.

Cliff Henderson kept wandering in and out of his thoughts. What Henderson had gone through Thursday night and Friday morning would have left most men in a bad way psychologically, but he seemed to have come through it without any visible scars. Strong, tough. Lucky. And still believing his father was innocent of Jenny Noakes's murder. He'd go to his grave believing it, just as Tucker Devries would go to his believing the opposite. No way of ever knowing which one was right, unless someday somebody confessed to the crime, and the chances of that were slim and none. Cold case. Cold forever.

"Jake?"

He blinked and moved out of himself, back into the warmth of the room.

"I need to ask you something," she said. "I've been thinking about it for a while . . . Maybe you have, too, I don't know. But I need to know."

"What is it?"

"Do you want to be with me?"

"I wouldn't be here if I didn't."

"That's not what I mean. I mean . . . in bed. Do you want to make love to me?"

The question surprised him. He didn't answer immediately; he wasn't sure what she wanted to hear.

"Be honest. Please."

"Yes," he said.

"You've never said anything, never tried . . ."

"It's not my call."

"Yes, it is, as much as mine. Do you want me? Despite my affliction?"

"I don't see you that way. Afflicted."

"How do you see me? As a woman or just a friend?"

"Both."

"A desirable woman?"

"In every way."

"You're not just saying that? Being kind?"

"No. You asked me to be honest. I'm being honest."

A little time passed. Then she got to her feet, single fluid motion, no hesitancy, as if she'd made a sudden decision. "I'll be in the bedroom. Give me five minutes before you come in."

"Bryn . . ."

"It's all right. I'm being honest, too."

He sat motionless, not thinking. When he sensed that it was time, he stood and went down the hallway to where the bedrooms were. Hers was dark; all he could see was the vague shape of her under the covers, the whitish shape of her face, her entire face. She'd taken off the scarf along with her clothes.

"Don't turn on the light."

"I won't."

"Come in here with me, but don't touch me. Not just yet."

He undressed, eased himself into the bed beside her. The sheets rustled—freshly laundered silk. The thought came to him that she'd put the sheets on especially for this, that she'd planned it.

They lay without touching. He could hear the slightly quickened sound of her breathing. And he was aware, then, of the faint, elusive scent of perfume—something else she'd put on just for him.

"All right," she said after a long, sighing breath. "But promise me you won't touch my face. Or try to kiss me."

"I promise."

She moved over, fitting her body against his in a shy, tentative way. The feel of her bare flesh was electric. Sensations stirred inside him that he hadn't felt in more than two years.

Colleen . . .

No. Bryn.

He made love to her as tenderly as if she were a virgin bride. Toward the end she clung to him fiercely, but even then she averted the left side of her face into the pillow.

Afterward, when they were breathing normally again, she clutched his hand in both of hers. "Jake? Was it awful for you?"

"My God, no. You know it wasn't."

"I was afraid you'd . . ."

"What?"

"Pull away. Be repulsed."

"Nothing about you could ever repulse me."

Soft sigh. Almost a relieved sigh. "For me, it was . . . I'm not sure I can put it into words. . . ."

"You don't need to. We don't need words."

Quiet.

"Hold me for a while," she said, "and then . . . go. Okay? I'd rather you didn't spend the night. I don't want you to see me in the morning. I'm not ready for that."

"Anything you say."

Her fingers tightened in his and she curled against him with her knees drawn up, like a child. He held her, staring into the warm darkness.

For the first time since before Colleen's illness, he felt at peace.

29

TAMARA

She kept waiting for Lucas to call, ask to see her again on the weekend. He hadn't said he would, but after all the fun they'd had together, she thought he might. Only he didn't. On Friday night she stayed home and hovered around the phone like a silly teenager, willing it to ring. Well, he'd told her his job required a lot of traveling; maybe he'd had to go out of town. Yeah, and maybe he'd had enough of her. She hoped that wasn't it, because she sure hadn't had enough of him. When you've been starving for close to a year and finally get a taste of it again, it takes a while to stop being hungry.

Saturday morning, she decided passive waiting sucked. He hadn't called her, so all right, then she'd call him. Twenty-first century, right? Women's lib. Lucas hadn't given her his home number, but he'd used her phone to call Mama before he left Tuesday night, to see if she got

293

home from her date, so his number was still on her speed dial. Detective Tamara.

She made the call, and on about the sixth ring a woman's voice answered. Thin, irritable, a little fuzzy around the edges. Must be sleep fuzz. Alisha wouldn't be boozing at eleven in the morning, would she?

"Is Lucas home? This is Tamara calling."

"Who?"

"Tamara Corbin. Friend of your son."

"He's a damn fool."

". . . What?"

Silence.

"Mrs. Zeller?"

"My name isn't Zeller."

". . . You're not Alisha, Lucas's mother?"

More silence. Then some hacking, wheezing noises . . . nicotine cough? "What do you want?"

"To talk to Lucas. Is he there?"

"No."

"Well, when he comes in, would you ask him to give me a call—"

"No," the woman said, and hung up on her.

Weird conversation. Lucas's mama or not? Not a wife, that hadn't checked out, but how about a live-in girl-friend? The scratchy, fuzzy voice hadn't been young, and those hacks and wheezes sounded like they'd come out of a pretty old throat. Well, she'd just have to wait for Lucas to get in touch to find out. If he got in touch. If he didn't . . . *c'est la vie,* it'd been sweet while it lasted.

The rest of the day dragged. Lonesome Saturday night

ahead. Unless Vonda and Ben were free and wanted to stop by later, share a bottle of wine, maybe go out to dinner at one of the restaurants on Potrero Hill . . .

Yep, they were and they did. So it wouldn't be a lonesome night after all.

At six o'clock the three of them were sitting out on the little porch that opened off the kitchen, just large enough for a table and four chairs, with a view of the backs of houses and apartment buildings on the next street over. The weather had improved, clear and windy today, but a mimosa tree gave the porch some shelter and it wasn't bad sitting out there. One of the perks of city living.

Vonda was showing now, really showing, and she was only five months along. She'd be big as a house before the kid was born. Boy or girl, they didn't know yet which it was, they wanted to be surprised. Vonda, who'd sworn never to get married and have kids. Pregnancy agreed with her, though; she had this definite earth mother glow. Ben agreed with her, too. Who'd've thought she'd hook up with a white Jewish guy after a string of about three hundred black dudes, and get knocked up and married and be so happy she glowed? Ben was a good-looking guy, Tamara had to admit that. And they were good together, they even *looked* good together. Even Vonda's racist brother James had seen that and quit giving her grief.

So they sat sipping Chardonnay and talking and the wine made Tamara mellow enough to want to spring Lucas on them. Casually she said, "Well, I met somebody last weekend. Took care of my little problem."

Vonda grinned. "Hey, girl. About time."

"Sunday night, Monday morning, Tuesday night."

"You ho! Why didn't you tell me sooner?"

"Hey, no big deal."

"Yeah, right, after almost a year. Who is he? What's his name?"

"You know him. Lucas Zeller."

It got cold out there all of a sudden. Ben and Vonda sat real still, staring at her like she'd just sprouted a second head.

"What?" she said.

"Oh Jesus, Tam. Not Lucas Zeller."

"Why not? Man was at your wedding reception, that's where I met him."

"Not by invitation," Ben said. He sounded grim. "James didn't know he was coming, didn't want him there."

"What's the matter with him, except that he's a mama's boy? He's been real sweet to me."

"He's on the down low," Vonda said.

"What! Come on now, you don't mean—"

"I'd never lie about something like that. James told me. Lucas tried to get him to join this club he's in."

Tamara stared at her, stunned. On the down low. Black men having sex with other black men, the way Vonda meant it. A group of switch hitters.

"No," she said. "No."

"When you slept with him, you made him glove up, didn't you? Every time?"

"Except the last, we ran out of condoms."

Vonda looked sick. "Oh God, Tam, you better get yourself tested. Right away, don't waste any time."

Lucas, on the down low. Every time except one.

Tested—

No!

30

Gregory Pollexfen spent less than eight hours in jail. His criminal attorney, an even more high-powered gent than Arthur Sayers, called in a favor and got him released on a minimal amount of bail.

That was the good news for Pollexfen. The bad news was that at eleven thirty Saturday morning, he suffered a stress-induced heart attack while cleaning up his library and was now in the intensive care unit at UCSF.

Joe DeFalco called to tell me the news. Quid pro quo. I owed him a favor, so I'd given him first crack at the story of Jeremy Cullrane's murder after Inspectors Yin and Davis carted Pollexfen away Friday morning. DeFalco is a look-out-for-number-one muckraker, but I'd known him a long time and he plays fair when he doesn't have a personal agenda.

"What's the prognosis?" I asked him. "Is Pollexfen going to make it?"

"Probably not. Long history of health problems, one of them a bad heart."

"Yeah, I know."

"Chances are he'll never stand trial for his crimes."

Not in this world, anyway.

On Monday morning I went over to Great Western Insurance to hand-deliver the agency invoice on the Pollexfen case. I also took along my copy of Barney Rivera's promissory note for the $5,000 bonus, just in case he'd forgotten offering it and putting the offer in writing.

Tamara had taken the day off again, but evidently not for the same reason as last Monday. She'd called Sunday night, said she wasn't feeling well, the flu or something; and if the listless, choked-up sound of her voice was any indicator, she was liable to be out more than one day. No problem for me to handle office business until she returned, just not this morning. Jake Runyon had a full schedule, so I'd brought Alex Chavez in to stand watch while I paid my visit to Great Western's chief claims adjustor.

Rivera's attactive blond assistant, Margot Lee, was at her desk when I walked into GW's claims department. She took one look at me and assumed a stiff, professional posture. I knew what she was going to say even before she opened her mouth—a parroting of what her boss had told her to say if I called or showed up.

"I'm sorry, but Mr. Rivera is unavailable without an appointment. He has a very busy schedule today."

"I'll bet he had a busy weekend, too." I leaned confidentially on her desk and winked at her. "The two of you have a nice time together?"

"I beg your pardon?"

"You and Barney. Go somewhere or stay in alone?"

"I have no idea what—Just what are you implying?"

"Don't worry," I said, "I'm always discreet. Mum's the word about the affair."

". . . *What* affair?"

"You and Barney, of course."

She had begun to look as if she'd just stepped out of cold storage; you could almost see the frost forming on her.

"Who told you that we were having an affair?" Frost on the words, too.

"He did, the last time I was here. Strict confidence, of course."

"I see. Exactly what did he say?"

"Oh, you know. That it was no big deal, just a casual fling." I winked again. "He said some, ah, very flattering things about you. Not too subtle, but still flattering."

"Oh, he did, did he? Well, it's not true!"

"No? You and Barney aren't—?"

"Certainly not!" She sounded as though she found the notion insulting, if not downright nauseating. There was heat in her eyes now and pretty soon it would melt the frost. When that happened . . .

"I'm going in to see him now," I said. "You won't announce me or try to stop me, will you?"

Ms. Lee said in an icy-hot voice, "I wouldn't dream of it."

The metaphorical needle I'd come here with had been about a foot and a half long. I figured it for double that length and rapier sharp when I went into Rivera's private office. When I came out again a few minutes later, I didn't have it anymore—it was puncturing his backside, all the way through both chubby cheeks.

There are satisfactions in this business, some greater than others. This one ranked right up there near the top.

7/23/09